Gangster's
Girl

A Gangster's Girl

Chunichi

URBAN BOOKS

www.urbanbooks.net

Urban Books
10 Brennan Place
Deer Park, NY 11729

ISBN-13: 978-1-60162-006-4
ISBN-10: 1-60162-006-3

First mass market printing: June 2007

Printed in the United States

10   9   8   7   6   5

Submit Wholesale Orders to:
Kensington Publishing Corp.
c/o Penguin Group (USA) Inc.
Attention: Order Processing
405 Murray Hill Parkway
East Rutherford, NJ 07073-2316
Phone: 1-800-526-0275
Fax: 1-800-227-9604

This book is dedicated to my loving mother, Angela McZeek, and my father, Gary Cobb. Thanks for your constant support and understanding. I love you both!

Acknowledgments

First and foremost I would like to thank God, for my ability to write is not a talent, but a gift with which He has blessed me. I credit all my success to Him. Without God, none of this would be possible.

Next I would like to thank Carl Weber and the Urban Books family for believing in my work and me. You have given me the opportunity of a lifetime.

To my parents: thank you, thank you, thank you. I could never thank you all enough. No one has supported me as much as you all. Thanks for your patience, your understanding, your unconditional love and never ending support.

To my little brother, Vincent McZeek, aren't you proud of your big sis?

Special thanks to my girlfriends. I love you all like sisters. Toya Duncan of TMD Design, your wit keeps me bright each day. Thanks for the unique designs. Sara Schaible of SOZO Fashion, thanks for keeping me on top of the fashion game. Meisha Camm, thanks for walking with me each step of the way. Chrissy Smith, thanks for introducing me to the "publication world." Lakicia Fortenberry, thanks for keeping me focused on what's important. Tracey Davis, thanks for being my big sister at heart. My lil' sis Tiffany Duncan, follow my lead. LaChele Edmonds, Melanie Camm, and Deetra Foreman, thanks for simply being the ones I exhale with.

Much thanks to all those who support me. Ricardo Burress, thanks for the constant push. When I am tired and frustrated you never let me give up. Deneen Majors of Major Creations Hair Studio, thanks not only for the bomb hairstyles but also for constantly promoting the book. My coworkers, thanks for listening to all my different scenes and answering the infamous "does this sound right?" question. Renee Bobb, thanks for showing me the ropes and for your endless advice.

Finally, a GRAND thanks to all those who doubted me and hate the fact I made it. You have given me the strength and drive to do it over and over again. This is just the beginning!

Prologue

How are you? My name is Ceazia (that's c-asia) Devereaux. It's 12:15 a.m. and I've spent the entire day in bed crying. I'm only twenty-five, but I have experienced as much as a 40-year *young* woman. Still, I am thankful, because those experiences have molded me into the great woman I am today. So sit back and sip an apple martini as I share my story.

At age 21, I was unstoppable. At five feet five-inches tall, 125 pounds, measurements 36-26-40, size six shoes and the caramel skin of a newborn baby, I lived carefree in a three-bedroom condo overlooking Waterside in Downtown Norfolk, Virginia. I felt on top of the world as I drove around town in my Lex coupe, labeled down in the latest Iceberg or Versace prints. Needless to say, I was hated by many and loved by few. But that was my motivation. The more they hated, the more I flaunted. As far as I'm concerned, hate makes the world go 'round.

My girls and I were the hottest chicks in the Tidewater area. Many *knew* of us, but not many actually *knew* us. They knew our names and faces, but that was about it. We were all "breeded beach girls". That's right, born and raised in Virginia Beach. We had the best of everything and never wanted for anything. When living with our parents we were only expected to do well in school during the week and attend church on Sunday. As long as we followed those rules, the rest was whatever we wanted. However, we were quickly hit with a dose of reality when we decided to move out on our own.

My dad was so furious about my decision to move out that he cut me off completely. He had plans for me to live at home until I got married, but the excitement of independence was just too much to bear. I had to move out on my own. Of course, I had a job and a comfortable amount saved, but that just wasn't enough to pay the price of being the shit! We had an image to maintain, and by all means, we were determined to do so. So, we began our female hustle. We decided to start a little side business of our own. With the help of our close associate, Cash, we were on and popping in a matter of days. Who had any idea that one could work only two days a week and bring in two grand?

Chapter 1

The Beginning of
the Hustle

It was my first day on the job, and I was nervous as shit. Although I wasn't sure if I would actually have the guts to go through with the date, I'd prepared very carefully for this day. I chose to wear my hair long and straight in order to accent the deep neckline of my black Versace dress. The dress was cute, yet classy, and my matching black sandals would add just the touch needed to emphasize my long, sexy legs. Of course, you know I had to splash on just enough Hypnotic Poison, my signature fragrance, to tickle the nose of those who passed by. I wasn't quite sure if I would have to drive, but in the case that I would, I got my car detailed and pulled out my wide selection of CDs instead of the typical reggae selection that usually blasts from the Alpine system. I was planning to make an impression—a big impression.

As I entered the lobby, I straightened my dress and adjusted my cleavage. I took a deep breath to calm my nerves as I pressed the number eight on the elevator panel. *I can't do this. I just can't,* I thought as I contemplated turning around and returning home. But there was no other option; either go on the date or be evicted. The more that realization set in, the more I hated my dad for cutting me off. I stepped off the elevator and walked into the very busy law office of Shaw, Glenn and Goldstein with my head high and breasts out. These were the best defense attorneys in town. They were notorious for defending all the big time drug dealers.

"Hello, my name is Ceazia Devereaux. I have a two o'clock appointment with Mr. Glenn," I said with a smile as I approached the receptionist's desk.

She advised me it would be a few moments, so I took a seat and glanced through the latest issue of *Vogue.* After about five minutes, a nice looking young man came in and sat next to me.

"How ya doin'? I'm Vegas," he said, extending his hand and speaking in an arrogant, yet sexy, tone.

He was cute but just a little too confident, so I responded by saying, "Is that Vegas as in Las Vegas or Garcia Vegas?"

"What you know about Garcia Vegas?" he asked while laughing.

"More than you, I'm sure," I replied.

"Is that so?"

Somehow, one word led to another, and we found ourselves still conversing five minutes later when he was called into his lawyer's office. I watched as he walked away, sporting his Coogi jogging set and fresh, wheat-colored Tims. His hair was cut close and had enough waves to make you seasick. He must have felt my eyes upon him, because right before entering the office he turned around.

"Yo, shortie, that phone on the table is for you. We're going out this evening. I'll hit cha later with the details." He winked, then hit me with the most mesmerizing smile. Before I could come to my senses and give him one of the sarcastic responses that I'm known for, the door was closing behind him.

Who in the hell does this nigga think he is? First of all, my name is not shortie, and second, he doesn't tell me we're going out, he asks me! And how is he just gonna assign a phone to me? He don't know me like that.

"Ms. Devereaux. Excuse me, Ms. Devereaux!" the receptionist yelled in an annoyed tone. I was so taken by Vegas that I didn't even hear her calling my name.

"Yes," I responded back, just as annoyed.

"Mr. Glenn will see you now."

I rose from where I had been sitting and advanced toward Mr. Glenn's office, but not before picking up my link to that fine, but cocky ass, specimen who had sparked my curiosity.

As I placed the phone inside my purse and walked toward his office, my stomach bubbled with fear. I entered the room and stood motionless, watching as he talked on his cell phone. The man before me was quite attractive in his navy Armani suit. He seemed to be in his mid-thirties. His skin was pale, hair was dark, and his eyes were green. He quickly wrapped up his phone call and gestured for me to have a seat. He suggested we stay in his office instead of going out for lunch. I have to admit I was a little disappointed, especially since I hadn't had anything to eat all day.

Just then, I noticed him closing the blinds, and I became even more nervous.

"Would you like a rum and Coke?" he asked. I let out a thankful sigh. I could definitely use a drink.

"Yes, please," I answered, nodding in the affirmative.

After two drinks and thirty minutes of idle chitchat, he was ready to get down to business. To be honest with you, so was I. His request was that I role-play as the wife of one of his clients. He wanted me to pretend we were discussing my husband's case and that he was threatening to quit in the middle of trial because he hadn't been paid. In what would be a desperate plea for him to stay on the case and clear my husband's name, I was to knock everything off his desk, climb on top, and start to masturbate, seducing him to the point that he would do what I wanted him to do.

After he finished explaining his fantasy, I stared at him with an incredulous look. *I can't do this*, I thought. This is not me. *I don't care how much I need the money. I just can't do this.*

As you may have already realized, I'm an escort, or at least I'm attempting to be an escort. This was my first assignment, and well, to be honest, I thought it would be easier.

Mr. Glenn must have noticed the hesitation on my face. He attempted to ease my fears by bringing up the subject of money.

"Look, why don't I pay you first? How does a thousand dollars sound?"

"A thousand dollars?" I replied. The agency said I'd only get two hundred fifty and that I was going to have to split that with them. Needless to say, one thousand dollars in cash was a great motivator. With that incentive, I knocked all the shit off his desk and slowly climbed on top of it, spreading my legs and lifting my dress. I moved my hand slowly down my stomach and toward my panties. I threw my head back and closed my eyes, moving my fingers in tune with the slow rotation of my pelvis. The whole time, thoughts of that sexy ass Vegas helped to get me in the mood. All I could picture were his waves and his pretty smile. As I moved my hand across my vagina, I imagined him caressing my body and kissing me softly. After a while, it was as if Mr. Glenn wasn't even there. I moaned as my hand became moist with my juices. I continued to envision Vegas slowly kissing my thighs as I ran my fingers across the ocean of waves he had for hair. I could feel his moist tongue enter my poonani and him sucking my clit until I moaned with pleasure as a signal of satisfaction.

Just then, something jarred me from my private interlude with Vegas and back into reality. It was the sound of Mr. Glenn moaning along with me. My eyes opened wide with surprise. I have to admit I was shocked beyond belief at the sight of him tugging and pulling on his little ass penis until his load shot out and dripped on my stomach, signaling the end of our date. I left in a hurry, feeling disgusted.

Once home, I adjusted the shower setting to steaming hot and then proceeded to scrub my body profusely, as if I could wash all the defilement I felt down the drain. When I finished, I lay in my bed and cried myself to sleep. I'd never felt so dirty in my entire life. The shower may have cleansed my body, but it sure as hell hadn't cleansed my soul.

Chapter 2
The Life of Mr. Vegas

I was dreaming. Dreaming about that fine ass Vegas I'd met earlier in the day. He was wining and dining me, taking away all the pain from the gruesome encounter with the lawyer.

Unfortunately, just when my dream was getting good, I was awakened by the shrill sound of my phone. I picked up, but only a dial tone greeted me. Then I heard it again, only the phone couldn't be ringing, because I was already holding it up to my ear. Now I was baffled.

What in the hell is going on? Am I still dreaming? I scratched my head, and then I realized what it was. It was the cell phone Vegas had given me at the lawyer's office. I scrambled over to my pocketbook and desperately emptied out my purse until I was holding the ringing phone.

"Hello, hello!" *Damn! No answer.*

However, that wasn't necessarily a bad thing. Although Vegas was cute and I desperately wanted to see him again, I didn't wanna seem pressed. And after looking at the mess on my bed, I realized that I had been a little too anxious to answer his call. Now, that would have been a big mistake because he would have heard the desperation in my voice. He'd call back, of that I was sure. Guys never gave up on me that easily. Besides, this would just go to show him that I wasn't sitting around anticipating his call. Self-confident guys like him liked the thrill of a little chase and challenge.

Since I was awake, I decided to call my girl, Meikell, and tell her about my first day at the service. I didn't really wanna relive what happened, but she was probably gonna call me soon anyway.

"Hello," Meikell's tired voice said.

"What's up, Mickie?"

"Nothin'. Just chillin'. How'd everything go?" Meikell asked eagerly.

"Horrible, but lucrative." I told her every detail of my encounter, from the thousand-dollar decision I had to make to the degrading joint mastur-bation experience with the attorney. Just the thought of his sperm flying in the air made my stomach turn.

Of course, Meikell, who I sometimes thought was crazy, responded by saying, "Damn girl, so now you officially a high-class ho."

"Was that supposed to make me feel better?" I said flatly, disappointed in the reality of the situa-tion. Just as I began to express to her how I was re-ally feeling, Vegas' cell phone rang again. This time I was determined to answer, so I ended my conversation with Meikell without as much as a good-bye. I'd just have to explain to her later.

"Helllllooo," I sang into the phone.

"Yo, C!" yelled a masculine voice.

This time I was on point with the sarcasm and responded with, "This is Ceazia. There's no C here. Who is this anyway?"

"Come on, now. You know who this is. That's why you sounding all sexy and shit, ma."

I don't know what it was about this nigga, but just the sound of his voice made me quiver. Give me a thug over a square any day.

"Look, I'm at the barbershop right now, but I'll be done 'bout seven o'clock. Why don't you pick me up at Granby and 27th around then?"

"You're joking, right?" I said.

"What, you ain't got no car?"

"I was just about to ask you the same damn thing," I retorted.

"This ain't about what I got. This is about if you gonna pick me up or not. So, what up, ma? You gonna pick me up or what?"

"Okay," I said without resistance, and he hung up.

I thought to myself, *Okay? Okay? You couldn't have thought of a better response than okay? You could have at least played a little hard to get. Any other nigga would have been shot down at the snap of a finger.* But this wasn't just any ol' nigga. He was so damn thugged out it was turning me on!

Sticking to my belief that first impressions make lasting impressions, I walked to my closet and pulled out the best. This time, I chose the newest Iceberg Snoopy print pants that were tight to perfection, and a matching fitted T-shirt. Like always, I wore matching boots with a Coach belt and bag. It was a little breezy, so I grabbed a jean jacket to complete the ensemble. As I walked to the garage, I patted myself on the back for having gotten the car detailed earlier.

It was about quarter after seven when I arrived at Granby and 27th, located in one of the roughest neighborhoods of Norfolk. I parked directly in front of the barbershop, which was one of the six storefront shops of the mini shopping complex. Like every shopping center in the hood, it consisted of a corner store, Chinese restaurant, barbershop, pager store, nail shop, and beauty supply store. Of course, fifty percent of the shops were owned by Asians.

There was much activity going on in the small shopping strip. Cars were playing loud music, an audience circled guys who were battling above the beats, and some guys just looked like they were up to no good, pacing and looking nervously back and forth. I noticed an obviously young girl who looked terrible for her age, asking a number of people for a dollar. After about five minutes of begging, I saw her approach one of the nervous guys, make an exchange, and scurry off like a little mouse. Call me naive, but it took a moment before it finally registered in my mind. The nervous men were drug dealers and the young girl was a fiend.

Oh my goodness, I just witnessed a drug deal!

Suddenly there was a knock on the door, and I almost jumped out of my seat. My hand went straight to my chest, as if to keep my heart from leaping out. When I nervously turned toward the knocking, I was relieved to see Vegas staring at me.

"What's up? You gonna open the door or what?" he asked.

"Oh my God, you scared me," I replied.

I unlocked the car and Vegas jumped in. Once inside, he directed me to an old house a couple of blocks away. The house was huge and looked as though it had at least five bedrooms. A long driveway led to a gated backyard. Parked in the driveway was a black Honda Accord with dark tinted windows and an older model Maxima. I was silently praying that the Honda was his. He quickly ran inside and emerged with a Nieman Marcus bag.

"You's 'bout a size six, right?"

"Yeah," I responded.

"And a European shirt 42?"

"Uh-huh," I said as he tossed the bag on my lap, nonchalantly.

"Well, this is for you."

I opened it, peeking inside, and then smiled a smile so broad that it showed all thirty-two of my pearly whites. It was my favorite—Versace! He was definitely on the right track now. I leaned over and kissed his cheek.

"Thanks, you didn't have to do this."

"You right. I don't gotta do shit. I just wanted to." He smiled. "You hungry?"

"Yeah, I could eat something."

"Then why are we still sitting here? Drive." With a huge smile, he reached down and reclined his seat.

Dinner was great. We ate at a nice little low-key seafood restaurant down by the oceanfront; it was a perfect choice since I love seafood. We ate a candle-lit dinner on the deck while admiring the stars and listening to the waves and the seagulls. It was so romantic, something I was not very accustomed to.

After eating, he suggested we take a stroll along the beach, talk a little, and get to know each other better. It seems like he only got to know me, because I did most of the talking. I was surprised that he was truly interested in things that were important to me, like my goals, school and work. I told him I graduated from high school as an honor student with an advanced studies diploma and that after high school I attended Hampton University where I received my degree in dental hygiene. He was pleased to learn that I had no kids and worked full time as a dental hygienist in a large dental clinic. When it was his turn to share, he told me that he was the youngest of three boys. He also had no kids but wanted some eventually. He was born and raised in the streets of Norfolk, repping Park Place to the fullest.

"How did you get the name Vegas?" I asked out of curiosity.

"I used to be a big gambler," he explained. "After a few big wins, my friends started calling me Vegas. Plus, I was living the lifestyle like those flamboyant niggas from Las Vegas."

As we continued to talk, I found out what effects my first impression had on him. He said my chestnut eyes originally mesmerized him. Then, when he saw how snappy my attitude was and how curvaceous my body was, he knew he just had to have me by his side.

After about an hour on the beach, he asked if I

wanted to stay at the oceanfront for the night. At first I was hesitant, then I thought *what the hell.* I didn't want to fuck up what may be a good thing by acting like Ms. Goody-two-shoes. Shit, I had done far worse before with people I didn't even like. So I agreed, and he chose the best hotel on the strip. He paid for the room and valet with no hesitation. Don't call him cheap.

Once inside the room, I took a seat in the small sitting area and flicked on the television while he showered. Emerging from the bathroom, he walked over to the Jacuzzi in the corner of the room, drew the water, and lowered his buck-naked ass inside.

I can't believe this guy, I thought as I admired his body through the mirrors surrounding the Jacuzzi. He had the build of a god! His ass and thighs were as firm as an NFL ball player's, his abs were rippled, and his man parts, well, let's just say, daaaaamm-mmn! It has got to be a crime!

"Want to join me?" he asked. "You can wear your panties if you're uncomfortable about getting undressed."

With a dick like that, nigga, I'm getting in ass naked! I thought. However, my response came out more like, "Okay, I'll be right in. You got to try to control yourself, though."

I undressed slowly as Vegas watched my every move in the mirrors. I was precise with each movement as I lifted my shirt and pulled down my pants. As I tempted Vegas with my tantalizing striptease, I could tell by the way he was licking his lips that he was enjoying the show. My breasts popped out with ease as I unsnapped my front closure bra. Because of the way his eyes were dilating,

I was certain that Vegas was quite pleased with my physique. Lastly, I slowly removed my butterfly thong and began to walk toward the Jacuzzi. I could see Vegas' dick rise as I stepped into the water. Little did he know I was just as pleased as he was.

Chapter 3
Girls' Night Out

The next morning, I was awakened by the shining of the sun through the crack in the hotel curtains. I glanced at the clock radio, which read seven o'clock. "Oh shit!" I jumped up shouting. "I'm gonna be late for work! God-damn it! Vegas, wake up! Wake your ass up!"

He didn't budge, but that was his problem. I was the one driving, and if he didn't leave when I did, that was just too damn bad. I searched frantically for my clothes as he slept like a log. Not able to locate my panties, I grabbed his underwear and threw them on along with my pants and shirt. Shit, guys have been stealing my panties for years.

Now, I know I was wrong for doing what I'm about to tell you, but I couldn't resist. Since he was sleeping so soundly, and since I was already going to be late for work, I decided, *Why not go through his pockets? A sistah's gotta know what she's dealing with, right?*

Like most of the thugs I've dealt with, Vegas

didn't carry a wallet. Therefore, I was able to locate his money rather quickly simply by digging deep. He had exactly thirty-five hundred dollars in one pocket and a little over a thousand in the other. As I continued my search, I came across a few phone numbers. One read Kim, then Steeze, and one was surrounded by little hearts and read Jalisa. I got a good laugh at that one as I ripped it up. I figured that he was pretty popular with the ladies from the way his pager was blowing up every five minutes the night before. It eventually got to the point where he had to turn it off. My biggest concern was that he might have been married. *God, I hope not.*

Last but not least, I came across his ID, which listed his name as Laymont Jackson and Virginia Beach, Virginia, as his place of residence. Now that was strange. I thought he was from Norfolk. Still, none of that was as confusing as his date of birth, which read September 17, 1980. At first I didn't pay it any mind, but then I realized he was younger than I was. That's when I started to do the mathematics and counted the years in my head. 1, 2, 3 . . . 10, 11, 12 . . . 18! *Oh, my God, this nigga is only eighteen years old!*

Just then, Vegas started to stir, so I quickly replaced the card inside his pants pocket. Part of me wanted to confront him about his age while the other part just wanted to have a good time, which was exactly what he had shown me.

"Yo, why you up so early?" he grumbled.

"Because some of us have jobs," I answered sarcastically. "I'm gonna be late for work. Now get up, Vegas."

"Fuck that shit," he responded very nonchalantly. "You wit' me. Chill out. Lie back down and get some rest. We were up late last night." He rolled over, trying to get comfortable.

What doesn't this nigga understand? I gotta get to work.

"Look, Vegas, I'm the only dental hygienist at a very busy dental clinic. I can't just stay home." I was quite perturbed at his previous statement.

"How much do you make in a week, ma?" He asked, rolling back over and staring at me.

"Not that it's any of your business, but I bring home about a thousand dollars a week," I snapped with attitude. I'd exaggerated the amount of money I made, but he shouldn't have been asking anyway.

"A'ight, I got you. Hand me my pants." I did as he asked and was surprised when he pulled out the smaller roll of money, counted off ten hundred-dollar bills, and handed it to me as if it were ten dollars. "Now come back to bed, a'ight?"

If I had known that was going to be the outcome, I would have told him I made twice as much. Not wanting to end my date with Vegas so soon, I agreed to stay. I called the office and used the excuse of a family emergency to get me out of a day of work. Then, I returned to bed and to the comfort of Vegas' arms.

Two hours later, we were up and on our way to Norfolk. It was the day of the Rap Concert '99, so I was happy that I had decided to take the day off. That way I would have plenty of time to prepare for the show. During the entire ride to Norfolk, Vegas was on his cell phone.

As a subtle hint, I sang softly with Aaliyah, "Your loooove is a one in a million. It goes oooon and oooon and oooon."

The way he laid it on me the previous night was definitely what I would call some one in a million loving. I must say, that was the best sex I ever had. And who would have ever imagined it would have come from an eighteen year-old? I have to give him his props, though, because if I had not come across his ID, I would have never known. He had all the characteristics of a grown ass man, including dick, body and mind. He actually had me screaming his name. Anyone eavesdropping would have thought I had hit the jackpot.

As I listened in on Vegas' cell phone conversation, I came to the conclusion that he was planning to have a meeting with this guy he referred to as Red. He also mentioned someone by the name of Martinez, but not a word was mentioned about going to the show that evening. I did wonder what all this "business meeting" stuff had to do with.

I drove Vegas to the same house we had stopped by the previous night. Before getting out of the car, he gave me the number to the cell phone he had given me at the attorney's office and told me it was mine to keep. He also slapped another thousand dollars cash in my hand.

I decided to give you two grand instead of one because I know you're going to that show tonight and may need a little extra pocket change." I thanked him and gave him a small peck on the lips before he got out.

"Damn! That's a fine ass nigga," I said as I watched him walk toward the house.

And generous, too!

When I pulled off, I immediately called my girl, Deedee, and made a hair appointment. I knew she would be booked up because she was the hottest stylist in the Tidewater area. Her services were in high demand. She even did cornrows for all the niggas in the area. She managed to squeeze me in. Then I called my girls to find out what the plans were for the night. I started with Tionna and then called Mickie and Carmin. The four of us always rolled together, though at times our clique could get as deep as eight girls. We all agreed to meet at Carmin's house at seven. That would give me enough time to get my hair done and purchase an outfit. Since I had a few hours before my hair appointment, I went home and freshened up. I quickly jumped in the shower and threw on a cute little Sergio jean outfit. After that, I hit the mall. I was able to find an outfit and get my nails done in record-breaking time.

After I got my hair done, I rushed to Carmin's house. Although Carmin is pure Italian, she is the blackest chick I know. Don't be fooled by the name. Her name should actually be Tameka. Carmin is knowledgeable in all the latest fashion and has a major in international design. She did freelance design for a number of artists and lived the life that many only dreamed of having. She knew all the hottest stars, went to all the celebrity parties, and even screwed a few of them too.

During her ideal life, Carmin had fallen hard for a new artist on the charts. The only problem was that the feeling wasn't mutual. He was involved in a relationship and had no intentions of leaving his girl. But as we all know, the power of the pussy can make a guy do some strange things. He claimed he loved his girl, but at the same time, he just couldn't stay away from Carmin. When he would go on tour to places like Europe, he would take Carmin along. He kept her laced in the finest fashions and even purchased her a Lexus SUV. Still, he stressed to her that he was not her man. That's the kind of shit that makes you wonder. You give a man your all—sex, head, and love—and he can't give you any type of commitment in return. And to beat all, he even had the nerve to be possessive. If he even thought Carmin was letting another nigga hit that, he would snap. However, if she saw him with his girl, Carmin had better not even think about cutting her eyes wrong or there would be problems. It takes a certain kind of chick to play the role as the other woman, and I definitely don't meet the criteria. I demand a certain amount of attention and to share it with someone else is just not possible.

Carmin was one of the wildest, coolest, most fun people you could meet. She had a gorgeous body with a waist and hips like Beyonce Knowles. She didn't have to put up with being second if she didn't want to. Not to mention she was voted MVP of the group when it came to giving head. With those qualifications, she could have any man on the entire East Coast.

Her two-bedroom apartment screamed her name. To most people, it would resemble a *Trading Spaces* project gone bad, but I thought it was the shit. She had a twist between eclectic and vintage furniture. Against the wall sat an old leather couch. It was a rust color with metal button accents around the arm. On her mantle were blown glass vases in cobalt blue and orange that held huge sunflowers. Her walls were bordered with pages from the latest fashion magazines. And my most favorite decorative piece of all was the portrait of Marilyn Monroe that hung on her living room wall.

Soon, everyone had arrived and we decided to have a couple of drinks, put on some Lil' Kim, the Queen Bitch, for some girl power, and spark one. The mixture of apple martinis, hydro, and the lyrics of *No Time* put us in the mindset we needed for the night to come. Tionna, the title holder for doggie style, was the comedian of the group. Our friends could always count on me to come in and form a comical tag team with Tionna. She drove a cute little bubble Camry that we often joked with her about. Not that anything was wrong with it because her shit was paid for, but it was just so funny when the rest of us had such elaborate cars. To understand the car, you must understand Tionna. Born and raised in New York, she never learned how to drive. We had just recently taught her to drive, and the Camry was her first choice for a car. Tionna was also the penny pincher of the group.

Now don't get me wrong, she had just as much loot as any of us, if not more, but the bitch was just so damn cheap.

After our drinks, we were ready to get dressed. We all put on our best because we knew the world would be watching. For some reason, all eyes of the area were always on us. It was four of us total, so we had to decide which cars to drive. We pretty much knew we could rule out Tionna's ride, therefore, we decided that Carmin would drive her Lex. We figured we all could roll in that together.

Once we hit the coliseum, it was on! Niggas were everywhere, and every single one of them was flaunting their jewels, cars, clothes and women. I was impressed with some of the chicks I saw.

"You have to be careful," Tionna quickly reminded me, "because if you don't, you could be fooled by the once-a-year show outfit."

She was referring to the girls who don't really have it the way that they would like to have you believe, but instead spend their whole welfare check on an outfit and accessories so they can be jiggie for the show. But catch them the next week and they are your straight up "Reebok broads."

Once we found a space, Carmin parked the truck and we headed for the doors. It seemed like we would never get there. We walked briskly as the wind whipped through our little outfits. Upon reaching the door, we found a line of at least seventy-five people waiting to get inside. Standing in line was out of the question, so we did like always and politely said "excuse me" to each person until we reached the front. We acted as though we were shareholders of the establishment. It's amazing how each person stepped aside without hesitation. I guess that's another benefit of being the shit and having a pussy. After three minutes of waiting, we were in and headed straight to the bathroom. In keeping with our girls' night out ritual, we had to put our hair in place and spray on a refreshing bit of fragrance. Afterward, we headed to the arena floor to check out the scene. Like at every show, there were your chickens, whores and hood rats, all trying to get backstage. There was no question we would get back there, though. Carmin already had things on lock.

We headed directly to the back and Carmin whispered in the security guard's ear. "Scratch my back and I'll scratch yours," she said.

Instantly, we were in. It's crazy how one simple phrase and a little sex appeal can go so far with men. As we watched the show from backstage, a couple of the artists started conversing with us. After a few minutes of chatting, they were ready to chill.

"Yo, y'all mad cool. Wanna smoke one?" one of the guys asked.

Wanting to be social, but at the same time not trusting any nigga, I responded by saying, "Yeah, we can spark one, but we'll roll our own shit."

They thought my response was real funny but decided to smoke with us anyway. We meditated on the herb for a while then decided we would depart. Before we left, though, I noticed Mickie and one of the guys exchanging numbers. I wondered why she would even waste her time, like there was any chance of them actually hooking up. Once back on the arena floor, we mingled with some of the ballers while Mickie continued to gather numbers. After a while, we made our exit.

The spot to hang after the club, show, or what have you, was always Fat Danny's Soul Food Restaurant. So, that's where we headed. Again, we walked right in and sat down, bypassing the line. This time things didn't go as smoothly, though.

We were only sitting for forty-five seconds before this terrible looking hood rat came over and said, "Hey, we've been waiting here for thirty minutes and y'all just walked in and took our seat!"

We all just looked at her and busted out laughing. She became very upset with our reaction to her statement.

"I bet your ass won't be laughing if I smack the shit out one of y'all bitches!"

And then it was on. Now, I would usually be the first to react to a situation like this, but this time, Mickie beat me to it. She stood up face to face with the girl and said, "If you a see a bitch, smack a bitch!"

Being from the hood, the girl was not about to back down. Instead, she challenged back.

"Cross this line, bitch," she said as she drew an imaginary line with her foot.

At that point, Mickie and I both looked at each other from the corner of our eyes to give a silent signal for attack. We both launched on her ass simultaneously. Immediately, her girls ran over to her rescue, but they got the same beatdown as she did. Tionna's New York instincts kicked in and out of nowhere a blade was produced. After a minute, blood was everywhere and we were out. We headed straight to Carmin's. The night was over, and what a night it was!

Once in the car, Mickie counted off, "One . . . two . . . three!"

"Friends are forever!" we all shouted together. We used this statement whenever we were faced with an issue and we came together as friends to overcome it.

On the ride to Carmin's, Mickie received a phone call. It was Cash. Cash was the manger of the escort agency we worked for.

"I need you for a job. Where you at, yo?" I could hear him yelling through the phone.

"I'm coming through the tunnel. Meet me at Ocean View."

We agreed we would never do spur of the moment jobs, but for some reason, Mickie agreed. I don't know about anyone else, but I found that quite shady. Still, we dropped her off and continued on to Carmin's. Later, we found out she was so eager because Cash had arranged a date for her with the rapper from the show.

When we got to Carmin's house, my cell phone rang. It was Vegas. I was surprised to hear from him so late.

"How was your night?" he asked sarcastically.

"It was alright."

"That's it, just alright? From what I hear you had a pretty exciting night," he responded just as sarcastically as before.

"What are you talking about, Vegas?" I asked, getting quite annoyed at the little game he was playing.

That's when he went on to tell me all about my night. I mean, he knew everything from what I had on, to us smoking with the rappers, to us fighting. I could not figure out how in the hell he knew this shit.

I know this nigga ain't psycho enough to follow me, I thought. *He's too damn cool for that.*

Not wanting to get into it with him while my girls were within earshot, and much too tired to argue, I decided it would be best just to end the call and deal with him later.

"We're at Carmin's, and I'm really tired. I'll holla at you in the morning."

"A'ight," he said flatly before hanging up and leaving me to stare at the phone in wonderment.

Chapter 4
Mickie's Hustle Struggle

A couple of months passed, and things between Vegas and me grew. Things were moving really fast. Vegas moved in with me and we planned to purchase a house the following year. We had plenty of room in my crib, but he still wanted a house. Really, the only thing he could complain about was the garage. He had two cars of his own plus my car, and my garage was only equipped for two cars. Not that it mattered, because his brothers were always driving one of his cars anyway. Speaking of cars, I was happy to learn that neither of those cars parked in the driveway of that big old house in Norfolk belonged to him. Vegas drove an Acura coupe for daily activities and his big boy Escalade for night excursions. Damn, that truck was tight! It turned me on from the first time I saw it. It was pearl white with mirror tint and 22-inch rims. The inside was equipped with five TVs, one in the deck, one in each visor, and one in each headrest. Of course, there was also a DVD player and PlayStation attached. The interior had upholstery made of beige leather. I swear, if that truck had a dick, I would have fucked it. Needless to say, that truck was his pride and joy.

Since it had been declared that I was officially Vegas' girl, a lot of things had to change. The first and most major was the escort job was out the door. There was no way his girl would be doing something like that. I had no problem giving that degrading experience up, though. Vegas had the best of everything, so he made sure I had it too. But the closer we became, the farther Meikell and I separated. Meikell seemed to think all the luxuries went to my head, and that's what eventually forced us apart. On the other hand, I thought she had become too involved with the side job and had changed herself. To her, it was no longer a side job. She made it her way of life. In fact, she quit her job as a director at a franchise daycare to escort full time. She talked, walked, looked and acted like a cheap whore. She wore wigs of every color, talked with ebonics slang, and dressed very distastefully. Cash was no longer just providing protection and setting up dates. He was now playing the role of her pimp. He had her fucking anything, including women, for little or nothing. The thought crossed my mind that she may have even been strung out. The word on the street was when she wasn't hooking, she was at the strip club trying to make a dollar. When I heard that, I decided it was time to have a heart-to-heart talk with her. She was my friend, and I wouldn't idly stand by and watch her destroy her reputation like that. Therefore, I called her.

"Yes, Mrs. Vegas," Mickie answered, obviously after looking at the caller ID.

"Mickie, I know things have been rough between us the last couple of weeks, but I'm calling to speak to you about the situation."

"Okay, so speak."

I knew Meikell was not going to make this easy for me, but I wasn't going to give up yet.

"Mickie, you really need to stop doing the side job."

"And why is that, Mrs. Vegas? Just because your life is so perfect now and you have all the things you want, you think you're better than me. Did you forget you were doing the exact same thing not so long ago? I'm sorry, C, but I'm not as fortunate as you are. I have to work for mine. Besides, it's not much different from what you're doing. I mean, you fuck Vegas, don't you?"

That was it. The little bit of compassion and concern I felt for her before went right out the window. I had to let that bitch have it.

"You know what? I was actually trying to help your ass out, but you're obviously jealous of me. So, do you. And just so that you know, niggas on the streets are saying you're hooking and stripping and all for small change."

"So what? Fuck those niggas and fuck you too." Click.

Those were the last words I heard before the dial tone began buzzing in my ear. I couldn't understand Mickie. Hooking and stripping? And where was the money going? She had the same crib, same car and same clothes. At least I cared enough to say something. Everyone else was just disassociating themselves from her. But after that last note, I was joining the disassociation group my damn self.

The closer Vegas and I got, the more things I began to find out. It seemed like his age wasn't the only surprise he had in store for me.

One day we were in the mall and out of nowhere this ghetto ass park chick comes behind us yelling, "Your son here! I know you hear me. Yo' son here!"

Vegas just kept walking, looking straight ahead as if he didn't even hear her. Now me, on the other hand, I had to see who the fuck this chick was just in case I was out one day and something jumped off. You can never be too careful with those park bitches. You just never know.

The more he ignored her, the more ghetto and louder she got. Vegas isn't the type that likes controversy, so he decided we should just leave. Of course, she followed right behind us. When we got to the car, she got in his face and said it again.

"I ain't got a damn son," he said back to her calmly. Then he stepped around her and closed the door to the truck. She stood there yelling in the middle of the mall parking lot, looking just like a damn fool. I folded my arms, rolled my eyes, and grinned in her face as we pulled off. But by no means was that the end of it. I had a thousand and one questions that I needed answers to.

"Your son? Your son? What the fuck was that about?" I asked in a tone that signaled I was about to lose it.

"She's a chick I was screwing while I was with my ex-girlfriend," he explained. "When I tried to cut things off, the bitch cried pregnant. So, to shut her up I gave her five hundred dollars to get an abortion. More than likely, she used the money to buy a new outfit. Mainly, those park bitches are only after the money. Now months later, she's hollering some shit 'bout the baby being here. I haven't even spoken to her since the day I gave her the money."

In my heart, I wanted to believe he was telling the truth, but simply responded by saying as I had said to his ass many times before, "Yeah, well, time will definitely tell. Just as time told that your ass lied about having no kids. When we first met, you told me you didn't have any children. The next thing I know, you got three."

Vegas did not speak. He just glanced over at me with that dumb ass blank expression.

"And now it's turned to three and a fucking possible!" I continued.

Vegas still did not respond. Instead, he just stared at the street and shook his head as he exhaled heavily. When I first found out about the other three kids, he said he didn't tell me about his oldest because he didn't think the kid was his. He never had a blood test. He just took the responsibility. And the other two lived in DC, so he thought I would never find out. He said that his reason for not telling me that he had kids was because I didn't have any and that I seemed like the type who wasn't trying to be bothered with no baby momma bullshit. And his ass was right!

Since I was now on a roll, I decided to ask another puzzling question. "And why do you have a Virginia Beach address listed on your ID?"

Finally, he opened his mouth.

"I lived there with my kids' mother and when I left her, she packed up and moved to DC with her family," he said with a pitiful ass look on his face.

With all the things I was finding out, I wondered what in the hell was next.

Chapter 5
A Sister's Deceit

It was September 17 and Vegas' birthday. I swung by to pick up Tionna and her little sister, Tonya, and then we headed to the mall. I purchased Vegas a Versace sweater, Versace jeans and some Durangos. It didn't take me long to figure out what he liked when it came to style. His taste was similar to mine. I guess that was just another reason why we were such a good match.

While out, Tionna bought her sister a few things. Tonya had been living with Tionna for a few months now. Tionna decided to take her in after their abusive aunt damn near beat Tonya to death. One night, she came in pissy drunk and accused Tonya of sleeping with her husband. When she confronted Tonya with her accusation, Tonya responded in a very snappy way by saying, "Maybe if you weren't drunk all the damn time, you'd be fucking your man and wouldn't be worried about me fucking him."

Tonya had a mouth that would make a preacher curse. So, you can imagine the effect it would have on an abusive drunk. That one simple statement caused Tonya to be bruised for a lifetime. The aunt beat Tonya until she was delirious. She beat Tonya with anything she could get her hands on, from a hanger to a phone to a chair. Not to mention all the punches and kicks that were included in that beating as well. By the time the police arrived, Tonya was unconscious and literally near death.

Of course, after that incident Tonya had to move out of her aunt's home, but there was no place else for her to go. Their mother was serving a life sentence for murder and their father was nowhere to be found. Their grandmother was already raising their younger sister and brother, so there really was no room for Tonya in her home, either. Therefore, Tionna fell obligated to move Tonya into the two-bedroom apartment that she shared with her boyfriend.

Tionna and her boyfriend, Shawn, were the happiest couple I knew. They had their ups and downs, but that's what made their relationship so strong. When Tionna met Shawn, he was in the Marine Corp. and quite demanding. After a night out with the fellas, he would come home drunk and start drama. He never hit Tionna, but he would do much damage around the house. Although he would not physically hurt her, he would verbally abuse her by calling her all sorts of names. His acts of rage got so bad that Tionna began to question if he was on drugs. After investigating, she found it to be true.

Tionna was furious when she learned that Shawn was occasionally sniffing heroin. She immediately kicked him out. Afraid of losing her, Shawn begged for forgiveness and asked her to get him help. Not wanting to ignore his cry for help, Tionna got him into an inpatient rehabilitation center. While in rehab, he began to explore the Muslim faith. It was as if he became a completely different person. He was much calmer and more sincere. His whole demeanor changed. He was just a humble man overall. Witnessing the change take place, Tionna decided to stick by him, and they made it through that difficult time together. Next to Jada and Will, they were one of the most committed couples I knew.

After shopping, Tonya seemed to be in a rush to get home, so we dropped her off, and then Tionna and I headed to the twins' house. India and Asia were new to the circle of friends, but no one would have ever known. They were both account executives at major banks in the area, and they both screwed their way up the corporate ladder to get those positions. Contrary to the way they were now living, they were raised as perfect Christian girls. Their father was a pastor and they had attended Christian schools. They still lived at home but were no longer those perfect twins that Daddy raised.

Asia had twins out of wedlock and was currently dating a guy who was married. India was a player in the cash exchange for all the major drug imports into the eastern coast of the U.S. Her fiancé was a kingpin out of Kingston, Jamaica. This guy was honestly the craziest muthafucker I have ever met. He had a tall, fragile frame, with dark skin, and eyes as cold as ice. He spoke with a deep voice and strong accent. Each time I saw him, I froze with fear. He had India under some sort of trance, but no one realized it except me. With my Creole background, I notice the power of voodoo very quickly. At times, it was as though India was not even herself.

India was planning to move and join her fiancé in Jamaica the following year. He told her that by then he would have reached his 2.5 million mark and would be ready to retire.

The drug ring that her fiancé operated had been passed on in his family from generation to generation. However, with that title came a lot of other shit that I didn't think India even knew about. I'd learned from firsthand experience. The guy Red, who Vegas dealt with, was part of the Dominican drug ring. I'd seen this guy fly to the States just to kill a nigga. He even had a little 90-pound chick that he would send at times to do the job for him. The shit was wild, and I definitely wouldn't want any parts of it.

As we sat and tripped out with the twins, Tionna's phone rang. It was her sister's boyfriend.

"Tonya had an accident! Get to the house quick!" I could hear him yelling into the phone.

We dropped everything and drove to her apartment in record time.

"Toooonyaaaaa!" Tionna screamed as she burst through the door, but there was no answer. We noticed Tonya's clothes strewn all over the living room floor and heard loud music coming from the direction of her bedroom. Tionna twisted the doorknob, but the bedroom door was locked. Out of panic, Tionna busted the door down and there was Tonya, completely naked, and she wasn't alone. Tionna's man was in there with her.

It was terrible. Tionna's face was filled with hurt and anger. She stood motionless, screaming as I rushed over to hold her. She resisted my hold and began to fight frantically as a half-naked Shawn approached her. I immediately pulled her from the house and into the car. This was truly a sad day for both of us.

Once Tionna calmed down, I took her back to my condo. I tried everything to make her feel better, but after such a traumatic experience, I knew it would be a long time before she healed. She had lost two people that meant the world to her. As we were talking about the situation, Tionna received another call from Tonya's boyfriend.

"Is Tonya okay?"

Tionna wasn't sure how to break the news to Tonya's boyfriend, and she sure as hell wasn't eager for him to experience the hurt and pain that she was, so she stalled for time by asking him a few questions about his earlier phone call to her.

"Exactly what happened to make you think Tonya was hurt?" Tionna asked.

I got a call, but when I answered, no one spoke,"

he explained. "I heard a lot of commotion in the background, though. I recognized Tonya's number, so I kept listening. There was a lot of tussling and moaning, like some kind of struggle. I started calling Tonya's name to see if she could answer me, but there was no response. I hung up and called back from my cell phone, but I just got a busy signal. I was afraid Tonya was hurt and just couldn't get to the phone. That's when I called you, 'cause I knew you could get there faster than me."

Tionna probed further to see if there was anything else Tonya's boyfriend could add to make the situation clearer. Unfortunately, there was not. She would never know what had really happened.

As Tionna and I resumed talking, Vegas walked in.

"What's up, baby?" he said as he kissed me on the lips.

"Nothing, honey, just comforting Tionna."

"What's the deal, T? No jokes today?" Vegas noticed Tionna wasn't her normal comical self.

"Nah, not today. I'm not in the mood, Vegas," Tionna responded in a daze.

"Damn, we can't have that. Why don't you ladies come with me? I'm gonna take y'all out. We can go to this spot on the oceanfront. I got one quick stop to make on the way, though. Is that cool?"

I don't know. I'm not really in the mood to be social," Tionna said.

"Aw, come on, you need to get out," I said. "Not to sound insensitive, but sitting around harping on the situation is not gonna make it any better. I know how hard it must be to cope with something like this, but putting yourself in an upbeat environment may be just what you need. If you don't feel any better once we get to where we're going, I'll have Vegas drop us back off."

After I finally got her to agree to come along, we all hopped in the truck and headed toward the downtown tunnel.

"Where we headed, baby?" It looked like we were going to Portsmouth, but Vegas hated Portsmouth. He would always warn me to stay out of Portsmouth because that's where the grimiest niggas lay. "I gotta meet my man real quick at the . . . the . . . umm . . . strip joint," Vegas said hesitantly.

"The strip joint?"

"Yeah, baby, don't trip. It'll only be a minute," he said as we pulled in the parking lot.

"Whatever! And your ass got exactly one minute too," I yelled as he was shutting the door.

Ten minutes passed and Vegas still wasn't back, so I decided I was going in after him.

"I'm going to get his ass, T. You coming?"

"I guess I better go, just in case you start wilding on a bitch."

We climbed out of the truck and headed in. The club was dark and smoky, the sounds of Luke blasting from the speakers. The DJ announced each girl as she entered the center stage. The girls danced, crawled, and climbed the pole while guys threw dollar after dollar on the stage. I searched and searched, but I didn't see Vegas anywhere.

Since he was so popular, though, I knew all I had to do was ask just one person in the establishment and they would tell me where he was.

"Excuse me, do you know Vegas?" I asked the bartender as I approached the bar.

"Yeah, he was just with Martinez. Hold on, I'll get Martinez to take you to him."

Martinez? I remembered hearing Vegas refer to a friend of his by the name of Martinez quite often, but I never met him. I was pretty certain this was the same guy, though.

The bartender finished serving a drink, and then shouted to a guy in the corner who was speaking to a nicely built female.

"Yo, Martinez!"

The guy walked over to the end of the bar and they began to exchange words. As they were speaking, Tionna and I walked toward them. The closer we got the more familiar the guy looked. We caught each other's eyes.

"Oh, shit. What the hell y'all doing here?" Cash asked nervously.

"I'm looking for Vegas. So, you're the infamous Martinez, huh? I had no idea. You do know that Vegas is my man, right? So, Cash, why does everyone else call you Martinez?"

"It's a long story, ma. Follow me. He's right in here speaking with my man."

We followed Cash to a room labeled VIP. In no way was I ready for the sight before me when he opened the door and we stepped inside.

"What the hell are you doing?" I yelled.

Tionna's mouth dropped to the floor as we

watched this trick suck dick in front of a group of men. She was oblivious to our presence as she continued to suck and stroke this guy to no end. As she was going down on the one guy, another was smacking her ass from behind. I could not stand there and watch any longer, so I walked over and snatched her by her head.

"What the fuck are you doing, Mickie? Get the fuck up!"

Needless to say, the guys were not pleased by my interruption.

"What the fuck you doing, shortie? We paid for this shit. What the deal? Are you trying to take over?"

Then, one guy actually had the audacity to grab my ass. At that point, Tionna and I both lost it, but before we could react, I heard a sound that resembled the cocking of a gun.

Click . . . click

The sound was enough to make everyone freeze. It was Vegas and he had his gun to the guy's head.

"You got a problem with your hands, man?"

I could see fear written all over the guy's face as he pleaded with Vegas. "Nah, Vegas. Man, I ain't know that was your girl, man. I'm sorry, man. You know I wouldn't disrespect you like that."

"Not only did you disrespect me, but you disrespected my girl. I think you owe her an apology," Vegas calmly responded.

The guy turned toward me with tears in his eyes. "I'm sorry, miss. I'm sorry. Please forgive me."

"His life is in your hands, baby," Vegas turned to me and said. "Do you forgive him? If not, he got to go. So, what's it going to be?"

I couldn't just stand there and let Vegas kill the guy simply because he had touched my ass. I mean, what he had done was disrespectful, no doubt, but I would live.

"I forgive him, Vegas. Let him go," I said while eyeing the nigga up and down as if he wasn't even worth the bullet.

Vegas lowered the gun. As the guy ran for his life, the front of his pants clearly showed how frightened he really had been. I looked over at Mickie as she grabbed her clothes and ran to the dressing room. Tionna and I followed closely behind.

"Mickie, why are you doing this? You are too good for this. You don't have to stoop to this level," I said.

"Yes I do." Meikell began to cry. "I don't have it as easy as you, C. I have to do this to maintain. I wish I didn't, but I do."

Tionna and I both hugged her as she continued to cry. There was no need to say anything more.

"You ladies ready?" Vegas yelled from the dressing room door.

"Yes, baby, we'll be right out."

We told Mickie we loved her and that we were sorry for isolating her. We hoped she would forgive us and that we would hear from her soon.

The ride home was rough. Once again, I had a thousand questions for Vegas.

"Why didn't you tell me you knew Cash?"

"You never asked," Vegas responded nonchalantly.

"So why haven't I ever met him? I mean, you always talk about him, but you never bring him around.

"You know I don't bring business to the house, Ceazia."

"I could tell by his tone that my many questions were starting to annoy Vegas, but that didn't stop me.

"So why did you have to meet at the strip club? Do you meet him there all the time?

"No, I don't. I meet him wherever he's at when I call, C."

"So why when I came in there you weren't with him? You were in the VIP room and he was out near the bar. If y'all were doing business, shouldn't y'all have been together?"

Running out of patience for my line of questioning, Vegas became angry. "Ceazia, if I was up to some shit, I would not have even brought y'all along. Damn, I was talking to Red about some shit that didn't involve Martinez, so we asked the nigga to step out. You don't know anything about the game, so please stop questioning me about how I run my shit."

"He's got a point, C. Cut him a break. Like he said, he was just handling his business," Tionna said from the back seat.

If I had been smart, I would have taken the advice of my friend and ended the conversation there, but I just couldn't. I needed more answers.

"Well, why didn't you tell me Mickie be up there doing shit like that? I'm sure you knew since you're so close to Cash.

Vegas' nose flared and he took a deep breath. "C, you're getting on my fucking nerves with all these damn questions. I can't know that man's hustle. That'll be like him trying to tell me who to sell my shit to. Shit, Meikell is a grown ass women. Maybe if you would mind your damn business y'all wouldn't be beefing now."

I can't believe this nigga is actually bucking on me like this. Vegas had truly violated.

He had touched a sensitive spot, and I reacted without thinking.

Smack!

"Who the fuck you talking to?" I yelled at him.

Skuuuuuuuurrrrrrrrr!

The screeching of the truck's brakes was the last thing I heard before Vegas grabbed me by the back of my neck.

"Bitch! I don't put my fucking hands on you, and I expect the same respect from your ass!"

"Okay, Vegas, I think you made your point! Let her go," Tionna begged while she pulled on his arm, trying to loosen his grip.

When he released his hold, I began to cry hysterically. I couldn't believe he put his hands on me. Needless to say, we didn't go out that night and the rest of the ride home was silent.

A few minutes later we arrived at Tionna's apartment. Still a bit shaken, I stepped out of the truck to give her a hug.

"I love you, girl. Keep your head up," I told her before kissing her cheek.

"I love you, too, and you do the same. From the looks of things, we're gonna need a *Waiting to Exhale* party," Tionna said with a small grin.

I gave her a slight smile in return as I climbed back into the truck. As we pulled off, I waved to her from the window and watched her disappear into the house.

When I got home I received a call from Tionna. She briefed me on the events that occurred after we dropped her off. Evidently, her time away was not quite long enough. When Tionna entered her apartment, she immediately noticed that Tonya's things were cleared out and her room was vacant. However, Shawn was not gone. He met Tionna at the door, his eyes red and filled with tears.

"Could you please leave? Take all your clothes and just leave!" she shouted, and then stood looking at him coldly.

Shawn could see how angry she was, so he did as she asked. He grabbed what he could carry and made a quick exit. After he left, Tionna cleaned the house and threw out anything left behind that was affiliated with Shawn or Tonya. After all she had done for *both* of them, she couldn't believe they would actually do something like that. She took her little sister in because she had no place else to go, and this was the repayment she got.

Not wanting to face all the hurt and betrayal that she was feeling, Tionna took two Vicodins and cried herself to sleep as she thought about all the events of the day. She just wanted the day to end. And what a day it had been.

Chapter 6
Tionna Faces Death

It had been almost a year since the incident with Tonya and Shawn, and Tionna was gradually getting better. She was seeing our therapist and making good progress. Charlotte is the therapist we had all consulted at some point in our lives. She was a young, white girl who knew her shit. It's unfortunate, but divas need therapy too.

Tionna was looking great. She had gone shopping and purchased new clothes. She got her hair done and her nails and toes, too. She even sported a new style. It was sort of funky, with a video chick swing. It was like old times. I had really missed Tionna during her deep depression. I was glad that my girl was back in the swing of things. That situation had really taken a toll on all of us. One evening, we all gathered at her house to celebrate and have a girls' night out, which we referred to as therapy outside of therapy. We laughed and joked as we thought about old times. Meikell brought her friend Linda and Linda's daughter, Shykema. Immediately, everyone noticed how Shykema resembled Asia's twins. Asia's daughters are named Shameah and Shakeya, and they are beautiful. They have gray eyes, long legs, and French vanilla skin, just like their father. We found it quite peculiar that Linda's daughter, whose name is quite similar, had green eyes, long legs and caramel skin. The curiosity was killing us all, so someone had to say something. India, the feistiest of the twins, spoke up.

"Your daughter surely resembles my nieces," she said in a sarcastic tone. She went on to tell Linda about her nieces and how her daughter's features were so similar.

"Oh, really?" Linda responded, "Well, Shykema's father named her. She looks *just* like him.

"Oh, that's interesting," India interrupted. "My nieces were also named by their father. So where is their father from?"

As Linda spoke, things fell into place and just as we all thought, Asia's twins and Shykema were sisters. Linda seemed undisturbed by the whole revelation. Asia, on the other hand, had the look of death on her face.

"Where were his standards?" Asia said, looking at Linda with disgust. "I mean, look at you and look at me. I'm a part of corporate America and you are just simply a disgrace to America."

To everyone's surprise, Linda responded very calmly. "I understand you're upset, but you shouldn't be. My daughter is two years older than your twins are, and besides, I have no contact with her father whatsoever. We didn't have much of a relationship. I met him at the strip club one night and we ended up having sex. Unfortunately, the condom broke and I ended up with Shykema. He ended up leaving right after her birth. We had some major conflicts of interest, if you know what I mean."

"No, I don't know what you mean. Why don't you elaborate?" Asia insisted.

"Not that it's any of your business, but I am no longer interested in men, so you really shouldn't worry." Linda responded in the same calm manner as before.

We were glad Linda responded the way that she had, because anything else would have been detrimental to her health. We all exhaled as the tension slowly left the room, and we continued to drink and trip out as before.

Asia was not worried that her twins' father would get with Linda. She was just upset that she didn't have any idea about his other child. Even though she hadn't known the twins' father during the time he conceived this other child, it still made her mad. It shouldn't have, though, because now he was doing ten years in federal prison. Asia was getting all his money and had a man on the side.

Just as we were leaving to go out, there was a knock at the door, which was quite surprising since all of us were already there. Tionna opened the door and there stood Shawn, looking just as pitiful as the day he left. In his hand he held a folded piece of paper. He handed Tionna the paper and left without saying a word.

Caught off guard by Shawn's appearance, she was nevertheless anxious to know what was contained in the letter. Tionna quickly unfolded the paper and stood silently as she read. Her eyes scanned the typed words.

Dear sir/ma'am:
   We have reason to believe you have come in contact with someone who might be infected with the HIV virus. Please report to your city public health department as soon as possible for testing.

"Nooooo! Oh God, no!" Tionna burst into tears. As we crowded around and read over her shoulder, we all cried with her. We could not believe this was happening. Things were so perfect, and now this. How could this happen to someone we loved so dearly? It wasn't fair. Tionna had only been with Shawn. They weren't using protection because they supposedly had a monogamous relationship. She never worried about getting pregnant because her doctors said she would never have children.

The next day, Tionna headed for the health department. The parking lot was filled with cars as she pulled up. With her head down, she walked in and handed the letter to the receptionist then looked around for a place to sit. There were chairs lined up in rows. The place was noisy and crowded. There were babies crying, mothers yelling, and nurses calling names every five minutes. She found a chair in the corner away from everyone and took a seat. She was afraid to get too close to anyone or touch anything because everyone, even the children, looked as though they were infected with some deadly disease. Tionna cried just at the thought of looking as bad as the people who surrounded her.

After a few minutes, the nurse called out, "Tionna Davis, exam room three."

Tionna walked into the exam room and the nurse advised her to get undressed. Once the nurse left the room, Tionna pulled off her clothes and put on the paper robe. A few minutes later, the doctor walked in. Exactly what Tionna did not want to happen did happen. The doctor was a man and he was gorgeous. Not exactly who she wanted to see as she was getting checked for HIV.

He explained that he would be doing an exam for STDs as well as taking blood to test for HIV. Tionna hated the pelvic exam. The feeling of that cold metal instrument was so uncomfortable. She tightened her muscles as the doctor inserted the cold speculum.

"Relax, honey," the doctor said while patting her knee. "Take some deep breaths and spread your legs." Ugh. She cringed at his words. Spreading her legs was what had gotten her in this mess in the first place.

She did what the doctor instructed and relaxed. It's funny how we women are always hollering about a big dick, but when they stick that speculum in us, we tighten our thighs and nearly jump off the table.

"All done," the doctor announced three minutes later. "I didn't see any signs of an STD. You will be contacted, though, once the blood results are back. I think I should also explain that just because you received the letter does not mean you are definitely infected."

Tionna sighed with relief. He actually made her feel a lot better. "Hey doc, if the test comes back negative, let's have dinner," she said and giggled to herself as she disappeared behind the curtain to get dressed.

His response was only a smile.

Tionna drove home in a daze as she wondered what the results would be.

A couple of days later, Tionna received another knock at the door. This time it was two detectives. She knew the day would come when they would catch up with India and come knocking at her door in search of answers. Tionna often broke into a cold sweat as she played over and over again in her mind the answers she would give to those questions regarding India and her involvement in the drug ring.

Nervously, she opened the door. As she looked the detectives in their faces, she wasn't sure what to say or what not to say.

"How can I assist you today, detectives?" Tionna asked, her voice shaking.

"Ms. Davis?" one of the detectives asked.

"Yes, I'm Ms. Davis."

"May we come in?"

"Sure. How can I help you?"

To her surprise, they wanted to speak to her about her sister, Tonya. She hadn't heard from Tonya or even spoken her name since the day of the incident.

"When was the last time you saw Tonya?"

I haven't seen her for some time now," Tionna answered.

"Do you know the names of some of Tonya's friends? What about some other family members who may have seen her?"

Tionna answered each question to the best of her ability while she waited patiently for a chance to ask her questions.

"What is this investigation about?" she asked once they allowed her the opportunity. She wondered if Tonya had gotten into trouble again or if she was missing or something. Before they could answer, there was another knock on the door. This time it was a social worker.

"This is Mrs. White from Virginia Beach's Department of Social Services," one detective explained. "She will be speaking with you as well."

Now Tionna was very confused and demanded some answers. "Exactly what the hell is going on?"

After suggesting that Tionna have a seat, the detective explained. "Tonya was recently murdered. We suspect Tonya's boyfriend and plan to charge him with the murder."

"Ahhhhhhh!" Tionna screamed out in pain.

Over the wail of her cry, the detectives continued to tell her the story of Tonya's death. "Once Tonya's boyfriend found out Tonya had been unfaithful he was infuriated. He called her constantly, demanding answers. Your sister eventually changed her number and he was no longer able to reach her. Our reports show at that point he began to stalk her."

"No!"

"There are numerous police reports filed by Tonya. There are reports about him following her from her friend's house, sitting outside the laundromat as she washed clothes, and even him sleeping in his car as she spent the night at her girlfriend's house. Things became more violent as Tonya's stomach grew and she became afraid for her life. She knew once her boyfriend found out she was pregnant by another man he would kill her."

"Oh, God! Nooo!"

"She eventually filed a restraining order with the Virginia Beach Magistrate. Unfortunately, that didn't stop the harassment. We learned from witnesses that a man named Shawn picked Tonya up from her doctor's appointment and they headed to his house. After a few hours, Tonya decided to go for a walk. As she closed the door behind her and turned around, her boyfriend stood there staring her in the face. He grabbed her by the arm, put a 9 mm to her back and instructed her to get into his car. They drove off and approximately three hours later, her body was found."

"Why?"

"He tied her to a park bench, molested her, and then shot her in the head. She did not die instantly. She died slowly as she struggled for her life."

As Tionna listened to the gruesome details of her sister's death, she felt like someone had just stabbed her in her heart. Her little sister was dead. She couldn't help but think that if she hadn't told Tonya's boyfriend what had happened that night, Tonya might still be alive.

The reason for the social worker's presence was that she wanted to speak to Tionna about taking custody of the baby.

"We were able to save the baby, but there are a few problems," Mrs. White said. "The father has disappeared and the baby may be infected with HIV." This was when Tionna knew for sure that the baby was Shawn's. They must have continued sleeping together even after she'd caught them and kicked Tonya out.

"There are currently no traces of the virus in the baby," Mrs. White continued, "but Tonya was diagnosed with the virus during her pregnancy. We would like to know if you would be willing to care for the child since you are the next of kin."

With all the things that were going on, Tionna asked for time to think things over. This was entirely too much to digest at one time. Honoring her wishes, they agreed to leave her alone and give her time to think through her decision.

Tionna drifted into another deep depression. She was not eating, sleeping, bathing or talking. She just lay in bed and wept. It was as if her whole world caved in on her. After three days of showing no improvement, we decided it was time to have

Tionna admitted to the hospital. She had lost five pounds during those few days. Her eyes had huge, dark rings around them, and her body was fragile. Her hair fell out strand by strand as we combed it. This was the worst we had ever seen Tionna.

When we arrived at the hospital emergency room, they asked her a series of questions regarding her health. She answered yes or no as they asked if she ever had a number of diseases. When they reached the question concerning HIV or AIDS, Tionna began to go crazy. She started yelling weird things, throwing things, and became very combative. Right when the doctors rushed in to control her, she began to have a seizure. They rushed her off through the double doors labeled TRAUMA and left us standing there in total disbelief.

We later found out Tionna had a nervous breakdown. The events in her life had finally taken a toll on her body. It was a struggle for her from the beginning. Her parents were absent during her entire life, and she had to take on adult responsibilities at a very young age. Then, the two people that she had invested so much love and time in betrayed her. A combination of those events, plus her fear of the possibility that she may have contracted HIV, her sister's death, and the guilt she felt for telling Tonya's boyfriend of her infidelity, were just too much for her body to handle. So, as a defense for the body, a nervous breakdown was triggered.

* * *

After a few weeks in the hospital, it was time for her to come home. We went to her home and cleaned it from top to bottom. We brought in fresh flowers, opened the windows, and made it bright and refreshing. We even purchased her a new bathroom and bedroom set. We turned her room and connecting bathroom into a tropical paradise. There were palm tree prints, plenty of plants, a relaxation fountain, and aromatherapy candles everywhere. It was beautiful. We felt that was just the atmosphere Tionna needed.

As we gathered her mail, we noticed a letter from the health department. We weren't sure if she needed to see it right away, especially since she was just recovering from her breakdown. We didn't open it because we were afraid that if the results were bad it would be hard to keep the secret from Tionna, who was so fragile right now. Therefore, we decided it would be best to hide the letter and give it to her when we felt she was capable of handing what could possibly be bad news. There was a letter from social services as well. We figured we would encourage her to read that letter just in case she decided to take custody of the baby.

Tionna was glad to get home. She was happy to see the house in such great condition. We all ate and laughed and enjoyed each other's company. Tionna was happier, but she still wasn't quite her self. After we ate dinner, she inquired about the mail. We handed it to her and she glanced at each envelope quickly.

"Is this all the mail?" she asked.

"What? That's not enough bills for you?" I said jokingly, and we all laughed—all except Tionna.

"Yeah, I was just expecting my test results from the health department," she responded disappointedly.

"We hid it, girl. We thought that maybe you shouldn't read it right away," India admitted, hating to see her in such misery. Then, she went to retrieve the envelope and handed it to her.

Tionna hesitantly opened the letter. After what seemed like an hour, Tionna began to cry. But this wasn't her ordinary cry.

"What does it say? What does it say?" Carmin asked impatiently.

Tionna responded very slowly. "Well it says . . . that . . . that . . . all my tests, well . . . they were . . . negative. There are currently no traces of HIV or STDs in my system."

For the first time in a long time, we were all happy. This situation brought us all together as one. It even brought Meikell back into the group.

"Guys, after all that we have been through, I have realized life is too short and that I need to make some changes. I'm going to give up escorting and dancing," Meikell vowed.

"You're making the right decision, Mickie. If you need anything, let me know. We're here for you," I said while smiling at Mickie to show my appreciation.

We all began to hug and cry. At that moment, we all realized anything could happen to any of us at any time. Life is too short and we should cherish those we have, because they might be gone tomorrow.

"One . . . two . . . three," Mickie counted.

"Friendship is forever!" we all shouted in unison.

Chapter 7
What Goes on in Cancun, Stays in Cancun

Two years had passed since Vegas and I first got together, so we decided to celebrate by taking a trip for two to Cancun, Mexico. The flight there was great. It was Vegas' first time flying and he was terrified. It was funny to watch the terror in his face as we loaded the plane and took off. I never saw him so afraid.

"Will you be having dinner and drinks?" the airline attendant asked once we were in the air.

Vegas shook his head vehemently. "No dinner for me. I don't think I can hold it. But I will take a Remy and Baileys." After his first drink, we began to drink shots of Quervo 1800. Before I knew it, Vegas was tore up and began yelling, "Shots for everyone."

His ass ended up buying the whole plane shots of 1800. Once we landed at the airport, things were chaotic. People were everywhere, yelling and reaching for our bags. We allowed one of the overly zealous guys to take our bags and lead us to the loading area. There were cabs, vans and limos waiting for passengers. We decided to go with the limo. On the way to the hotel, Vegas drank a Corona. The Coronas there were huge! They were in black bottles the size of champagne bottles.

Once at the hotel, we checked in and headed directly to our room. The room resembled a small apartment. There was a separate area for the living room and kitchen, and through the French doors was the bedroom. Attached to the bedroom was an enormous balcony that overlooked the ocean. We could see everything on the beach. The balcony was equipped with a table, two chairs and even a blind we could pull down to block out the sun and add privacy. The bathroom had a standing shower and a whirlpool tub. There was even a telephone on the wall beside the toilet.

As soon as we finished a tour of the room, we stripped naked and got into the Jacuzzi. We relaxed and sipped on the complimentary bottle of Dom P that was placed in the room prior to our arrival. Thirty minutes later, we heard a knock. It was room service with our order. We indulged in a seafood feast. The dinner consisted of everything from mussels to octopus. It was delicious.

By nightfall, we were at the pool. The pool was quite unique. It was like a miniature tropical rain forest. It had a waterfall pouring over a cave, palm trees scattered about, and a bar at the poolside. We didn't even have to get out of the pool to get a drink. Beside the bar, there were cement stools built into the pool bottom. We decided to have a few more shots of 1800. This would bring us to a total of seven for the day, not counting the champagne we drank with dinner.

As we sat at the bar, I noticed a young woman dropping her bikini top and teasing a few men at the bar. When Vegas looked over, she began to lick her lips and jiggle her breasts at him. I became infuriated! *Oh no the hell this bitch ain't!* I guess she could tell by the look on my face that I was not pleased with her actions.

"Perdona me. I did not know he was tu hombre," she said in broken English while looking at me.

I did not respond. Instead, I just rolled my eyes at the hussy as I turned my attention back to Vegas and we downed the shot that sat before us. After another, we both became quite frisky. We were in a hurry to finish our drinks so we could return to our room for some passionate lovemaking. Right before we drank what we said would be our final drink, Miss Titty Jiggler came strutting over.

"May I join in your next shot? The next one will be on me."

Of course we accepted the free round, and we all drank up. After the shots, we all became more relaxed and began to chat. We learned that the young lady's name was Arizelli and she was from Brazil. Her skin was like a rich, creamy caramel, and her hair was long, black and silky. She had a tall, slim build. The Quervo must have gotten her frisky as well because she began to get very friendly with Vegas and me. She was constantly playing in my hair and rubbing my back as we talked. She eventually directed us to a secluded area next to the pool.

"Your breasts are so beautiful," she complimented me. At that point, she untied my bikini top as well as hers. The alcohol must have been having a bigger affect on me than I realized, because no way under normal circumstances would I have allowed another woman so much control over my body, not to mention my man.

She motioned to Vegas. "Go ahead, touch them. What do you think?" Arizelli invited.

He touched them and compared firmness.

"They're both nice and firm," he said.

"Well, don't you want to compare taste?"

Vegas took her up on the invitation and began to caress and lick our nipples. He massaged our nipples until they rose and then licked each one until they were covered in the wetness of his tongue.

"Do you guys smoke ganja?" she asked. We both nodded our heads in the affirmative. "Well then, let's go through the waterfall to the cave and smoke a blunt," Arizelli suggested.

We followed her in there, and sat and smoked until we were super nice. The weed and tequila mix had us horny as hell. Vegas and I began to kiss and undress, forgetting Arizelli was even there. She helped undress us both and caressed our bodies as we kissed. As Vegas went down on me, she licked and caressed my nipples tenderly. Then Vegas lay down and I began sucking him madly. She grabbed my waist and started grinding against me gently. Next, she got on her knees and licked my womanhood from behind. After a while of this, I yearned to feel Vegas' manhood deep inside me, so I mounted Vegas slowly. The whole time, Arizelli was right behind me, squeezing and moving along with me as I rode him into ecstasy. He moaned and grabbed Arizelli's ass as we exploded together.

The next morning, we woke up bright and early and headed for the booze cruise. It was a small cruise ship with an all-you-can-eat buffet and an open bar. The ship was to take us to a private island, which had more food and drinks. Everyone was wilding out! It was so wild that they did not allow cameras or camcorders on the boat. As we passed an area on the way to the private island, the tour guide told everyone to throw money into the water and make a wish and it would come true. Many of the people were throwing coins and a few people threw dollars, but Vegas was so drunk that he started throwing fives, then tens, and then twenties. Soon, he was throwing fifties and people began to jump off the boat after the money. We were weak with laughter watching those crazy ass drunks. The captain stopped the boat, fished out the dummies, and then asked that no one else throw money.

Once we got to the island, Vegas and I decided to partake in some of the available activities. We rode Jet Skis, went horseback riding and parasailing. Parasailing was the worst! Vegas threw up everywhere. After we took a moment for him to compose himself, we went snorkeling. I hated it.

In fact, I didn't even want to get in the water. There were fish everywhere. I hated the feeling of them flapping all over me. After a few minutes of panicking, I finally got it together. We followed as the guide pointed out all sorts of colorful fish and coral.

"Don't get too close to the coral," he warned. Unfortunately, his warning came a bit too late.

"Oh shit! I'm cut!" I had gotten a little too close to the coral and ended up with a number of cuts and scrapes. I was bleeding everywhere. Then I heard someone yell something about a shark. I almost shit in my thong.

"Vegas! Help! There's a shark and I'm bleeding. Don't let me die," I cried hysterically as I swam toward him. I could see the shark at the bottom of the ocean. I thought for sure that I was going to die.

"Calm down, everyone," the guide shouted. "There is no need to panic. This type of shark only eats from the bottom of the ocean."

Vegas looked at me. "I know this nigga don't think we buying that shit. That's why their asses always the first ones to be eaten. Come on, baby, let's go."

With those words, Vegas and I hauled ass back to the Jet Ski so that we could head toward shore.

Beating Vegas to the Jet Ski, I said, "I want to drive, baby."

"Girl, you know damn well you don't know how to drive a Jet Ski."

"But I never tried. Please, baby?" I begged.

"Go ahead, but be careful."

We climbed on the Jet Ski and I started it up. I decided I would ride around a little while before going to shore. I didn't do well at first. I was afraid to go too fast, but I knew I had to give it more gas in order for it to move. However, I was still hesitant.

"Give it some gas! Go!" Vegas yelled, getting frustrated.

Starting to get pissed at all his damn yelling, I ended up giving it too much gas, and we shot off toward the ocean going at least 50 miles per hour.

"Slow the fuck down, girl!" Vegas yelled as water splashed in our faces from the waves. I was just starting to get the hang of things when I hit a wave.

"Ooohhhhh shiiiiiiit!" is all I heard as Vegas went flying off the back of the Jet Ski. The engine was smoking and I couldn't start it back up. I sat there laughing as he floated in the middle of the ocean with a terrible grimace on his face. He didn't find a damn thing funny at all. Within a few minutes, the guide came over and pulled Vegas out of the water. Then they came to get me, and took us back to the shore. Once on shore we occupied one of the small huts and blessed it. We laid down our beach towel and rolled up a fat one. After a few puffs, my bikini was off and sand was everywhere as we had hot, sticky sex. A few moments later, it was time to load the boat and head back to the hotel. Once back at the hotel, we decided to call it a night, exhausted from the day's activities.

The next morning, a little Mexican lady awakened us. "Buenos dias, senorita! Housekeeping!" she yelled from behind the door.

I sat up and my head was spinning. There was

no way I could make it to the door, so I just yelled back. "No, thank you! No housekeeping!"

I was praying she would understand. Evidently, she did, because she placed a tray at the door and left. After a few more hours of sleep and a morning's dose of Alka Seltzer, I was able to get up. I got the tray from the door. It consisted of a newspaper, towels, fresh flowers, and a breakfast menu. We ordered brunch and ate on the balcony as we watched the various activities on the beach. There was volleyball, and a beach party thrown by the hotel. We decided to go and check out the beach party. I wore a gorgeous, tropical print string bikini. As the finishing touch, I wore a small wrap around my waist. Vegas wore Versace swimming trunks and black, Italian leather Versace flip-flops.

On our way to the party, we ran into Red. Now, wasn't that a coincidence? To say that I was surprised to see him would be an understatement. However, Vegas didn't seem the least bit surprised. They walked over to the beach bar together and chatted as I sat at a nearby table. A few moments later, Vegas approached me.

"You mind if I step out for a few hours, baby?"

Although I was a tad bit irritated at Red's presence, I agreed. I wasn't sure what it was about Red, but I just did not trust him. For some odd reason, I would sometimes have thoughts that he might try some shady shit and I'd have to kill him.

Not wanting to attend the party solo, I returned to the hotel room to get some much needed rest. A few hours later, Vegas returned, loaded down with bags. He bought me Prada and Gucci sneakers, a Dolce & Gabana swimsuit, a Louis Vuitton bag, and two pair of Pradas for himself. I was so thrilled with the gifts.

"Thanks, baby! You are the sweetest person ever," I cried with joy. I was already overwhelmed by the trip, and the gifts just made it all that much better.

He must really love me, I thought. As a way of showing my appreciation, I pleasured him with an hour of passionate sex.

After making love, we made another attempt at heading to the beach party, which was still in progress. We arrived just as they were having the Shake-What-Cha-Momma-Gave-Ya dance contest. Women crowded the stage as the DJ played "Lap Dance" by the Nerds.

"Ooh baby, you want me?" The girls on stage yelled as they danced provocatively.

The way they were shaking, gyrating and degrading themselves, you would have thought the prize was more than just an off brand bikini and a bottle of Cristal. The men went crazy as the girls began to take their clothes off. I noticed Vegas inching his way toward the stage. He glanced back at me for approval.

"Go ahead, baby. Do you," I said, smiling.

He was surprised at my response but didn't hesitate to head straight for the stage. One by one the judges began to eliminate girls. The closer they got to the final girl, the wilder the show became. Pretty soon, the girls were all butt naked. When they got down to the last two, it was downright terrible. They were doing anything in a desperate attempt to win.

One girl pulled Red on stage, laid him down,

massaged his penis, put her breasts in his face and bounced on his dick to no end. All this was done while she was naked! Her butt jiggled like Jello and her boobs bounced like balloons as she went up and down. When it was time for her competitor to perform, she was determined to win. All morals and values were out the door. Butt naked, she grabbed a girl wearing a string bikini out of the audience. She lay on her back with knees bent, and pulled the girl from the audience on top of her in the same position. The girl from the audience lay on top of her, back to breast, with her legs straddled outside of the competitor's.

The competitor massaged the girl's breasts with one hand, while caressing the clit with the other, all the while their bodies moved together. Then out of nowhere, Red's drunken ass jumped in front of the girls, dropped to his knees, threw their legs up, and began to pump them wildly. Needless to say, the competition was over. By a unanimous vote, the "liberal lesbian" won. The bottle of Cristal was popped and poured all over her. The crowd went crazy as the women bathed in the champagne and licked it from each other's breasts. What a waste of some good ass champagne! After their show, they both ran into the beach water and the party moved there. Vegas, however, quickly made his way back over to me.

Looking at each other in disbelief, we laughed and said in unison, "What goes on in Cancun, stays in Cancun!"

* * *

The next day, it was time to head home. I had a great time, but I was ready to go. Believe it or not, I had started to get homesick. We arrived in Norfolk about seven P.M. and were home in no time. As we approached the door, Vegas noticed that it was cracked.

"Shhhh, be quiet," he whispered. "Hold on. Don't go in."

He pushed the door open a little and I managed to catch a glimpse. My condo was trashed! Furniture was turned over and stuff was everywhere. The anger must have been written all over my face because Vegas immediately put his hand over my mouth.

"Shhhhh. Don't say shit."

It took all I had to keep from screaming. He rushed to the car and retrieved his gun from the trunk.

Just as Vegas entered the house, the burglar stopped in his tracks, standing right before him. Vegas held fire as he looked the young guy in his eyes. He recognized the teen as one of the young runners from out the way. He knew the kid was working for someone else so he decided to spare the kid's life. He had a better plan for payback in store.

In a matter of seconds, the kid ran out through the French doors. We looked around but found nothing missing. A lot of my furniture and expensive paintings were destroyed, though. I never thought I would need my homeowner's insurance, but that incident certainly made me thankful I had it. After examining the condo we went to the garage, and that's when I lost it. I certainly wasn't keeping quiet then.

"My car! My fucking car!" I yelled at the top of my lungs as tears welled up in my eyes. My pride and joy had been vandalized! They stole my rims, my TV from the dash, my system, and destroyed my interior.

"I'm calling the police!" I yelled while searching through my bags frantically for my cell phone.

"No!" Vegas snatched the phone from my hands. "Look at this house. It's obvious this was a drug burglary. If we contact the cops, all it will do is make our spot hot. Don't worry, baby. I'll handle this shit."

After Vegas convinced me not to contact the police and assured me he would take care of things, I calmed down somewhat. Then I noticed a very worried look on Vegas' face.

"Baby, what's wrong?" I asked.

"I feel responsible. I should have never brought this shit around you."

Even though none of Vegas' associates ever came to our home, he still felt like the break-in happened because someone thought he had money or drugs in there. He pointed out how the burglar searched in odd places like the toilet, washer and dryer, under the mattress, and in the closet paneling. These were places people would normally hide drugs or money. Not to mention there were plenty of things in the house worth stealing and those things weren't even touched.

We called the insurance company, locked up, and headed to a hotel at Waterside. Once we were checked in and settled in our room, I questioned Vegas.

"Baby, why didn't you shoot when you saw the burglar?" I was certain my man was thugged out, so I knew it couldn't be because he was scared.

"Well, I recognized that lil' nigga who broke in our crib," Vegas explained. "He's too young for me to bust up, so I got another plan. Now get dressed. Dress comfortably and wear dark colors. You're coming with me."

I did as Vegas instructed and followed him out to the truck. We drove to one of his boy's houses and traded off the truck for one of his cars. Vegas mounted a pair of 30-day tags on the car.

"You ready, baby?"

"Yes, I am," I responded eagerly showing my man I could be his down ass bitch.

"Well, jump in the driver seat," Vegas said as he handed me the keys. He lay on the floor in the back seat and directed me to the location of the guy's hangout. Once I reached the area, Vegas pointed him out.

I drove up to the group of guys and said, "Excuse me. Do any of you guys know where Berkley is?"

The young kid who had robbed us was the first to respond. This was working out perfectly. "Yeah, it's about five miles away." He started giving me detailed directions. Pretending to be confused, I used my sex appeal to persuade the young boy to get into the car.

"That's a lot for me to remember. Do you think you can ride with me out there? I'll pay for a cab to get you back, or you can just stay at my crib if you like."

Hearing exactly what he wanted to hear, he jumped right in with no hesitation. He had no idea what was in store for him. When he got in, I immediately hit the lock. Vegas sat up quietly and put the gun to the back of the guy's head.

"Look straight ahead. If you turn your head in either direction, I will blow your fucking brains out. Got it?"

"I got it, man . . . I got it," the terrified little boy said.

Vegas knew the boy was working for someone. "Who in the fuck sent you to my house? I know yo' punk ass don't have the balls or the brains to come up with that shit on your own."

The guy was so scared that he told Vegas everything. "Man I'll tell you everything. Please, just don't kill me. Niggas on the streets is hating, man. They mad 'cause you got all the parks on lock. Bear paid me to break in and steal yo' stash and money and shit. I wasn't trying to do it, man, but I had to do it to clear an old debt I had with him. Come on, Vegas, it's part of the game."

With those last words, Vegas became infuriated. "What, bitch?"

Pop . . . splat!

Vegas pistol-whipped the young boy in the head. Blood splattered against the car window.

"What the fuck you know about the game? Lil' nigga, you don't know shit. Have you moved any keys? As a matter of fact, have you even seen a key? What about raw? Have you even had any raw? You been on this corner for years, man, pushing nick, dimes, and caps. You ain't shit, nigga. You haven't even entered the game, bitch."

After a little more terrorizing and a spit in the face, Vegas let the guy go. He put so much fear in that little boy's heart, he would never think of crossing Vegas again.

Chapter 8
Holiday Celebrations

After the break-in, Vegas didn't waste any time buying a new house. We paid off the balance owed on my condo and quickly moved into our new five-bedroom house in Church Point. We lived near all the stars, from entertainers to athletes. The house was gorgeous. It was on the water and surrounded by a huge wrought iron gate. There was a three-car garage and a huge backyard. In the backyard was a deck with a gazebo, a boat ramp with his and hers Jet Skis, and a large pool.

The inside of the house was like a small palace. Our bedroom was separated into two sections. The first room had a huge bay window with a beautiful view of the water and was equipped with a Jacuzzi in front of a fireplace. The other section of the bedroom consisted of our bed, closet and bathroom. Our TV rose from the foot of the bed at the push of a button, and our walk-in closet was the size of a small bedroom. The closet had a rotating rack and compartments for shoes, hats and bags.

The bathroom had a standing shower separate from the tub. The tub had a built-in whirlpool. There were also his and hers toilets and sinks. The living room had a huge, vaulted ceiling with skylights, a marble floor, and a beautiful fireplace.

The entrance of the house opened to a winding staircase on each side that led to a loft overlooking the living room. We even had a theater room with a wall projector and surround sound, a weight room where I could practice my shadow boxing, and laundry chutes in each upstairs bathroom that led directly to the laundry room.

Before we knew it, summer was over and it was my birthday. We were spending so much time working on the house that we hadn't had time for anything else. So, when Vegas suggested that I should take the day off on my birthday, I agreed.

By noon, we were out of the house. We jumped in the truck and he blindfolded me. He drove for about fifteen minutes before stopping. Then, he helped me out of the truck. After helping me take a few steps, he removed the blindfold.

"Oh my God! Oh my God! I can't believe it!" I screamed. "Thank you! I love you so much!"

I jumped up and down for joy like a kid on Christmas day. I couldn't believe it. It was my dream car. When I originally mentioned it to Vegas, he told me it was out of our price range.

How did he do it? I wondered.

In front of me sat a red Lexus SC 430 with a huge bow around it. I had been in love with that car ever since the first time I saw it. Immediately, I jumped in. The interior was all white leather. There was a single TV in the dash, 20-inch Sprewell rims, light tint and a fully customized system.

"Follow me to the Lexus dealership," Vegas said as I adored my new car.

When we arrived there, I ran into my ex boyfriend. This guy had treated me like shit our entire relationship. He knew I depended on him for so much during our relationship, so he used it to his advantage. There were times he would try to make me feel obligated to do certain things because I needed him so much. With all these things in mind, I was happy that this time I was the one shitting on him. He had a stinking look on his face when Vegas and I drove up. I just smiled at him and walked right past as if I didn't know him. Once I got over to Vegas, I pointed out my ex-boyfriend. Vegas looked at him and laughed.

"You used to fuck with *that* wack ass nigga?" He couldn't believe someone like him had me gone.

Still laughing, Vegas walked off and talked with an older white guy for a few minutes before handing him an envelope. Then, the white guy handed him an extra key and the title.

There is no way Vegas purchased this car in cash, I thought. But I wasn't about to ask any questions.

I was one of the first people in the area to own that car, so you know I had to shine. I pulled up in front of all the hottest clubs in the area full speed so the Sprewells would keep spinning when I came to a stop. That was the shit! It looked like I was floating on air when I would pull up.

The more I adored my car, the more my conscience would eat at me. I loved my car, but I still wondered how Vegas was able to afford it. So, I did a little research of my own. It turned out the white guy at the dealership made a little business trans-action with Vegas, and that's how he was able to get the car for me. At that point, I knew there wasn't anything Vegas wouldn't do for me.

Christmas followed my birthday. I purchased Vegas a two-way pager, an X-Box game system and an earring so big it could have made him part of the Cash Money Millionaires. It was platinum and covered in princess cut diamonds. He bought me a red mink and some matching red alligator boots, which he special ordered from the Mauri catalog. They were knee-high with pointed toes and graphite stiletto heels. But the best gift of all was my puppy!

"Oh, my goodness!" I said as I burst into tears. He bought me the cutest tan cocker spaniel.

"Her name is Prissy. She reminds me a lot of you. I hope you like her."

"I think that name suits her perfectly," I said as I picked her up. She wore a diamond collar with the name "Prissy" around it.

Later that night, it was time for the Annual Baller Christmas Gala. This was like the Players' Ball, but with a gangsta twist. This was the time for all the area ballers to show off their girls, jewels, clothes and rides. Vegas wore a deep royal blue mink, match-ing gator boots and belt, and a mushroom-colored suit underneath. I wore a dress of the same blue that dipped in the back to just above my butt crack. The front was sheer, and my private parts were covered only by a small rhinestone design. It was gorgeous.

We pulled up to the red carpet that lay in front of the hotel and stepped out of the stretch Mercedes. I must say, we were the hottest couple there. The party was off the hook! The music was great, and they gave out all sorts of door prizes. They gave away a DVD player, surround sound system, and a TV. One girl even won fifteen hundred in cash.

Throughout the night, I noticed a number of the local hustlers whispering in Vegas' ear. "Look, man, give me a call so we can do some business," they would say. Amongst those was a hustler who went by the name of Bear. He wore a gray suit with pink gators and a matching scarf on the outside of his suit coat. Bear had no idea that Vegas knew he paid the young punk to break into our place.

"Vegas! What's up, baby?" he said as he dapped him up. "How you doing, Miss Lady?" He said as he gave me a seductive smile. I didn't speak. I just smiled slightly.

Bear turned his attention back to Vegas. "Shit is rolling on the streets, man. What cha gon' do? I'm trying to get you on my team, nigga." Vegas arranged to do business with Bear.

"Baby, why are you talking to him like everything is cool?" I asked after Bear walked away. I didn't understand why Vegas would work with someone who had set him up.

"It's all part of the game, baby," Vegas explained. "It's safer that way. I prefer to keep my enemies close."

After a night of socializing and showing off, we headed home, pissy drunk. Vegas couldn't keep his hands off me during the ride home. The slightest touch was turning me on. My head was spinning as I lay back with my legs cocked open. Vegas buried his head between my legs, making me moist with every kiss. He pleased me exactly as I imagined he would when I masturbated in the lawyer's office on my first escort assignment. In fact, it was even *better*. His tongue was wet and warm inside me. I grabbed the back of his head as I came in his mouth.

By the time we reached home, we were both drained beyond belief.

New Year's followed right behind Christmas, of course. Instead of celebrating, Vegas had become quite annoyed over the past few days. It had been months since he had heard from Red. We were straight living off the stash, and he was worried about what the future would bring.

"I think you should get your mind off money for a while, baby. Let's go to DC to celebrate the New Year," I suggested, sensing his frustration.

He agreed and we headed to the club. We arrived at about eleven o'clock New Year's Eve. The club was packed. The line was wrapped around the corner. In front of the club was an entourage of nice cars lined up for valet parking. The valet parking was provided only for a selected few. I'm not sure what made us so special, but I guess our abundance of cash flow had a lot to do with it.

As we approached the entrance, a huge, dark guy said, "A hundred dollars starting here."

Vegas paid the man and we headed straight to the VIP room. Once we entered the VIP room, we sat at a table and the waitress ran over.

"Hey, Vegas! What are we having tonight?" The boney little waitress asked as she smacked on her fruit-flavored bubble gum. Vegas ordered a bottle of Cristal to pop after the countdown and a few drinks for us to sip on until then.

With only seconds until the start of a new year, we all began the countdown.

"5, 4, 3, 2, 1 . . . Happy New Year!"

Bottles began to pop everywhere. We clanked our glasses together in a toast and followed it with a long, passionate kiss. Confetti dropped as the DJ played *Auld Lang Syne* and everyone sang along.

"I love you, baby. And as long as I walk this green earth, you'll never have to worry about anything."

"I know, baby. I love you too." I wondered what Vegas was thinking as he spoke those words.

While everyone celebrated, Red walked up. Was it me, or did it seem that he always popped up at the wrong time?

"I gotta holla at you, man. Take down my new number and hit me up," he said in Vegas' ear. Vegas took out his phone and entered Red's number, then Red left.

We partied for another hour before heading for the hotel. We were extremely drunk, damn near to the point of having to hold each other up, as we waited for the valet to bring our car around.

"What the fuck is this?" We heard a woman yell from behind.

We turned around and there stood Vegas' baby's momma. She was all in his face, yelling and screaming.

"You all the way up here and you can't even call or try to come see your kids?"

Not wanting a confrontation and especially not wanting her to ruin what had been a perfect evening so far, I grabbed for Vegas' arm and said, "Come on, honey, our car is here."

That must have really upset her, because she turned to me and pulled out a blade. Before I could react, Vegas grabbed her and slammed her against the hood of the car.

"Bitch, you done lost yo' damn mind!" He strangled her and continuously banged her head against the hood of the car. He was choking her so terribly that her eyes began to roll to the back of her head. I could hear her gasping for air. Vegas wasn't himself. His eyes were cold and still. I was afraid he was going to kill her. I began to yell frantically.

"Vegas, baby, please let her go! You're going to kill her, baby! Let her go!" It was as if he had been taken over by some sort of demon. I begged him to stop as the police rushed over. They immediately tackled him to the ground face first. I cried hysterically as they cuffed him and placed him under arrest. I followed them to the police station so I could immediately post bail. I waited hours in the cold jail before they informed me he would not be released.

* * *

The next day, I headed home alone. The ride was long and horrible. I was tired and worried. I arrived home around four in the afternoon. As soon as I walked in the doors of our big, lonely house, the phone was ringing. I rushed to answer it.

"Hello . . . hello?"

"You have a collect call from—" the operator began to say. I immediately accepted the call. It was Vegas.

"What's up, baby?"

I was so happy to hear his voice.

"The charges were dropped, but I'm being transported back there for probation violation because I was out of state. I spoke to Bear and we came up with a way to continue business. I'm going to need your help, baby."

I knew Vegas wouldn't be able to get things done without me, so I agreed. "I got you. Just tell me what to do."

"Just keep a lookout for the mail," he said.

In a couple of days, I received a letter from Vegas with instructions. I was to be the backbone of the plan. It was my job to get the product and give it to his brothers. Once a week, I would meet Bear and pick up the raw heroin. I would spend hours in the basement mixing the product to form a missile that would blow the fiends' brains. I had to be sure to add just enough cut so that the dope wouldn't be weak. Once my mixture was right, I would fill the caps one by one. Normally, Vegas would have someone else do the capping for him, but he didn't trust them enough to send me to them alone. Once the package was complete, his brothers would sell them by the bundle and give me the money as they pumped it.

Vegas was expedited to Norfolk jail a few days after I received the letter. He was convicted of the violation and sentenced to sixty days. Just as he instructed, I picked up the product once a week. After a while of this, I began to notice Bear coming at me incorrectly. One day when I went over to his home, he had the lights dimmed, music on and drinks out.

"Why don't you stay and have dinner with me?" he suggested as he grabbed the package.

"No, thanks. I'm in a hurry," I said, aggravated.

"Okay, but you're missing out. You really look nice today. That outfit really complements your body."

"Thanks, but I have to go," I said curtly.

Eventually, I couldn't take it anymore. I had to tell Vegas, and planned to do so when he called later that night.

"Hi, baby."

"What's up, ma? You sound stressed."

I was hesitant to tell him, but I did. "Baby, Bear has really been saying some slick things out his mouth. When I go over, he procrastinates and does all sorts of things to try to make me stay."

"Did he touch you?"

"No, baby, but I'm starting to feel a little uncomfortable."

I'm sorry you have to go through this, baby girl," Vegas said sincerely. "I told you I would never let anything happen to you, and now this nigga is violating. Don't worry, ma. I got this, when I get out in two weeks. I owe that nigga anyway. Make the pickups as usual."

Click.

In two weeks, my baby was finally home. It had been hard, but I held the fort down. I took him to the basement and lifted the cement block to expose his money all wrapped and stacked: $300,000 dollars exactly, and not a penny off.

"Damn, girl." His face lit up. "You handling shit, huh? Charlie B ain't got nuttin' on you. You that down ass bitch that niggas dream about."

He gave me a bear hug, lifting me off my feet, and followed it with a big, wet kiss. But things weren't over yet. He had a little unfinished business to take care of. Bear had crossed Vegas for the last time and he wanted to set shit straight.

After dinner, we talked about it.

"Baby, I can't let shit ride. Bear has crossed me for the last time. I got something for that nigga, but I need to ask for your help." Vegas had that cold stare on his face once again. I knew it could only mean one thing . . . death. Still, I loved my man so I agreed to help him.

No one knew Vegas was home, so I made arrangements for the next pickup as if nothing had changed. I met Bear at his house about eight P.M. Once again, he had set the mood for lovemaking.

"Why don't you come in?" he asked. "I cooked seafood, your favorite."

This time, instead of declining, I played along.

"Sure. What did you cook?" I said while walking in.

"I cooked boiled snow crab legs, shrimp, lobster, broiled fish, and linguini."

We ate dinner and drank champagne at a candle-lit table. After dinner, he dimmed the lights and we moved to the couch to watch a movie. Suddenly, Bear felt very sleepy. I sipped on some Moet as he laid his head on my lap. Bear had one of those huge remotes that controlled nearly everything throughout the house. I pressed a switch and instantly the lights were off. Within minutes, he was asleep.

Zzzzip . . . smack!

Bear woke up unable to move. "What the fuck is going on?"

"You had your head in the place I lay my dick at night," Vegas replied calmly. "If you don't want dick in your face, don't block my spot. "

I could have died from laughter. Vegas had actually unzipped his pants and smacked Bear in the face with his big, black dick. Bear's head was spinning and within a few minutes he was out cold again. Those pills I had slipped in his drink really had him delirious. I knew he was out of it, but I was still concerned that he might remember bits and pieces of the night once he came to.

"Baby, what if remembers it was us that did this to him?" He'll kill me, Vegas." I began to worry.

"He won't remember anything, C. Come on, don't be getting all scared on me now. I thought you were my lil' Charlie B. And besides, I've told you a thousand times that as long as I'm around you don't have to worry about shit. I got you, ma. I got you."

We robbed him of all his stashed dope and at least fifty thousand in cash. Then we took a few other things to make it appear like an actual break-in had taken place. Before we left, we placed him in the tub, hog-tied with tape.

The next day, word was on the street that some-one had broken into Bear's house. It was amazing how the story changed. The word was Bear had taken some bad Ecstasy and was robbed by some chick he was dealing with. Bear thought one of his close friends was suspect. No one had any idea it was Vegas and me. Vegas laid low for a few weeks then finally announced that he was home. Shortly thereafter, Vegas received a call from Bear.

"What's up, man? You know some bitch set me up. You hear anything about it while you were in 811?" That was the name everyone used when re-ferring to Norfolk City Jail, because the building's street address is number 811. Vegas kept it short and gave him some bogus story.

"Man, that shit really got me fucked up in the game," Bear continued. "I'll probably be out for a minute. I'm gonna hook you up with my man so y'all can keep shit flowing."

A few weeks later, Vegas hooked up with Bear's connect and he was back in business.

"Baby, you aren't dealing with Red anymore?" I asked, realizing that I hadn't heard Vegas mention him in a while. That's when he let me in on the conversation they'd had on New Year's night.

"Red told me he had been out of the country taking care of business for the past few months but to give him a call so we could hook back up. I'm skeptical about that though, ma. I think I'm just gonna cut that nigga off."

I was happy with that decision because I always felt Red was up to no good anyway.

Chapter 9
Anniversary Perks

It was March and our third year anniversary. Vegas had planned a wonderful night out for us.

"Hello."

"Hey, baby, dress nice and be ready by seven. I'm taking you out."

I didn't waste any time preparing because I knew Vegas would have something special planned. I wore a black dress with the front open down to my belly button. It was long, with a single split to my upper thigh. I wore my hair up with large, dangling diamonds, a wide diamond bracelet, and a small belt with a rhinestone buckle. My purse was a small clutch bag with rhinestones.

"Happy anniversary, baby," he said, coming in the house dressed to impress and handing me a dozen red roses. He followed the words with a small kiss on the lips, being careful not to smear my MAC lip gloss.

Vegas wore a light green suit, a green mock

neck shirt and dark green gators with a matching belt. My secret spot began to get moist just from his appearance.

Damn, he looks so good, I thought as I got a whiff of his Versace Blue Jeans cologne. I loved it when my man dressed up, and it must have been clearly written on my face.

"Get your mind off sex, baby. We got a long night ahead of us. You've got plenty of time to get this dick," he said as he smacked my ass.

I placed the flowers in a vase on the living room mantle and we headed out. He took me to a downtown upscale restaurant. He had reserved the basement room for us. The setup was gorgeous. The cook came in and offered suggestions from some of the selections that were on the menu. He gave me so many options that I couldn't make a decision, so he decided he would bring me a healthy sample of all the seafood entrees.

We ended up having a four-course meal. We started with a Caesar salad, spiced onion soup, and garlic bread. Then, we ate oysters for an appetizer. The main course was wonderful. It was the best seafood I've eaten. It consisted of clams, lobster, shrimp, and calamari. We sipped a house wine as we ate. After dinner, we had a sample of a number of desserts.

After we finished, Vegas excused himself for a few minutes. When he returned, he was followed by what seemed like the entire restaurant staff and patrons. He walked up to me and got down on one knee.

"You have been there through the ups and

downs. You had faith in me when no one else did, and you have proven to me that you are down with me no matter what the situation. So, I have to ask you with all the love in my heart . . . Ceazia Devereaux, will you do me the honor of being my wife?"

"Yes . . . Yes, Vegas, I will!" I replied as I burst into tears.

The whole room erupted with applause as he placed the ring on my finger. It was a platinum ring, with a 3-carat princess-cut diamond and baguettes in a cathedral setting. It was a perfect fit.

"Thank you, baby. From this day forth, I send my love, and it's up to you to receive my heart," Vegas said in the most sincere way.

I will, baby. I will," I said through the tears. This was indeed the happiest day of my life.

After dinner, we boarded a yacht Vegas had chartered for a little cruise. The cruise was romantic. The music was soft and the night was cool. We walked to the top level outside the boat and danced slowly to the music. Vegas held me tightly as he whispered in my ear.

"I love you so much, girl. I'm ready to spend the rest of my life with you."

We kissed passionately. Vegas bent me over slowly and I clutched the rails of the boat as he ran his hands up the split of my skirt. The feel of his hands running up my thighs was instant stimulation. Vegas lifted my skirt slowly and slid my panties to the side. I moaned as he gently inserted his penis into my vagina, which was now dripping wet. I was briefly taken away by the moment as I moaned with passion.

When the cruise ended, we went home. In the bedroom I had placed rose petals, and candles all around the Jacuzzi. There were strawberries with melted chocolate and a bottle of Cristal in an ice-filled bucket beside the Jacuzzi. I figured there were only a few things you could give a man who already had everything, so I had to get creative.

I gave him all the pleasures a man could desire. I started by giving him a full body massage, then I fed him strawberries and let the warm chocolate drip over his body. I licked the chocolate from his chest and stomach. Next, I performed for him. I danced erotically and used toys as I performed. I covered a dildo with whipped cream and licked it up and down before inserting it into my vagina. After my performance, Vegas was ready for the sex of his life. We made love in every position, including anal. After hours of lovemaking, I brought out his gift. I had purchased Vegas a multicolored Jacob watch. Each section was colored, with a matching diamond bezel. It was the hottest watch on the streets and all the rappers were sporting it. He was very pleased, to say the least.

"Damn, baby! You're spoiling me. Where the hell you get money for this shit? You been digging in my stash?"

"Baby! You know I wouldn't touch your money!" I said as I playfully punched him in the chest. I don't think he realized that I had been saving all my checks. Since we were living together, I didn't have to pay anything. He covered all the bills and bought me everything I needed. As a result, I ended up accumulating a huge savings.

The next day I immediately contacted the crew to tell them the news. Everyone responded with the same excitement I felt when Vegas proposed. That is everyone except Meikell. Carmin and Tionna argued over who would be the maid of honor, while India demanded I choose bridesmaids dresses that complemented her boobs and play reggae at the reception so that she and her Jamaican mate could win' to the Caribbean tunes. Asia, on the other hand, was only concerned with the budget. Meikell didn't seem enthused at all. Although we had squashed our differences a long time ago, Meikell still seemed a bit jealous. Instead of congrats and best wishes, she gave me warnings and cautions. Nevertheless, I was happy and couldn't wait to spend the rest of my life with Vegas. Our anniversary was great, and not even Mickie could ruin such a wonderful day.

The next couple of months were great. Business was wonderful with the new connect and Vegas was on a roll. As I dressed for work, I stood naked in front of the mirror and asked, "Do you think I've gained weight, baby?"

Vegas walked behind me and looked in the mirror.

"Yeah, that *ass* is getting kinda fat," he said as he smacked my butt.

I'm serious, baby. It looks like I've gained a lot of weight."

"Okay, okay, let's see." He paused while he took a closer look. "On the real, your ass and your titties are growing, babe, but it's cool. You look nice like that."

Vegas loved it because I had more butt and my breasts were huge. But I was concerned that I might be losing my hourglass figure. However, when my period didn't come, I knew there was more to it. I went to the doctor and sure enough, I was pregnant. I was ten weeks along and carrying twins. I guess all that anniversary sex had planted something in the oven. I couldn't wait to tell Vegas the news.

"Baaaabyyyyyy!!!" I sang as I walked in the house.

"What's up?" Vegas responded.

I walked into the bedroom, but he wasn't there.

"Baby, where are you?" I yelled, anxious to tell him the good news.

"I'm in the weight room. What's up, ma?"

I quickly headed to the weight room and opened the door. The room reeked with the smell of sweat, but the sight of Vegas' perfect body laying horizontal on the weight bench instantly caused my juices to flow. I stood at the door motionless as I adored the sight. His legs were open and I could see the imprint of his penis through his 76ers jersey shorts. His shirt was off and his body was covered with beads of sweat. His body was screaming my name.

"What's up, baby?" he asked again as he wiped the sweat from his face. I was so turned on I had forgotten what I wanted to say. As he rose to a sit-

ting position on the weight bench, I walked over to
him and straddled my legs over his. Vegas immediately lifted my lavender Coogi dress and ripped off
my g-string. I guess all the lifting had him pumped.
I untied the string behind my neck so that my now
huge breasts flopped out. Vegas lifted them one by
one and licked my nipples.

"What . . . did you . . . want to . . . tell me?" He
mumbled between licks. He slipped his penis inside me in one swift motion. I was so aroused I
could barely speak. Just as I felt an orgasm coming,
I yelled it out.

"Baaabyyy! We're having a baby!"

The room fell silent and Vegas lifted me off his
penis.

"What did you say?" Vegas asked.

"We're having a baby. Vegas, I'm pregnant, with
twins."

"Damn, baby! When did this happen? How
many months are you? Are they boys or girls?"
Vegas asked question after question. He was ecstatic. He had everything except a family. I guess on
our anniversary I ended up giving him something
that he didn't have after all.

I immediately called all my friends and shared
the news. Everyone was just as ecstatic as Vegas.
Again, everyone with the exception of Mickie. But
just as with the engagement, I refused to let her
rain on my parade. Vegas and I were the first couple in the circle to have a child, which added even
more excitement to the good news. Tionna would
have been, but she couldn't bring herself to adopt
the child that her sister and ex-boyfriend had cre-

ated together. It was just too hurtful. The child would have been a constant reminder of the deceit, her sister's death, and the HIV attached. The child was diagnosed with HIV after all. Nevertheless, we were all excited to finally have a baby within the group.

As the days passed, I grew bigger. I was pregnant and proud. I couldn't wait for five months so that I could begin to shop. I had already chosen names: Anaya and Zanaya Serene Jackson. They would share the same middle name. I didn't bother choosing boy names, because I was sure I would have girls. Vegas didn't care either way. He was just happy that I was having his child, or should I say children.

I spent each day watching *A Baby Story, Maternity Ward,* or reading parenting magazines. I often looked at interior design magazines for ideas for the twins' bedroom. It was a battle between Pooh and sleeping teddies for the theme. Of course, I couldn't even work on that until after five months. This self-imposed five month rule was really killing me. There was so much that I wanted and needed to do.

I figured since Vegas and I were going to have a baby, there needed to be some changes. I wasn't sure how he would take it, but I wanted him out of the game. I figured we could start a business to keep the flow of money coming in. We had plenty of money on hand, as well as a whole lot invested. Asia made sure we all invested our money as it came in. She was like the Suze Orman of the group. That's how she earned the title Ms. Money-bags. I decided it was time for me to discuss my decision with Vegas.

"What's up, baby?" Vegas said as he answered the phone.

"Vegas, we need to talk. Can you come home right away?"

"Yeah, ma. There's nothing wrong with the twins, is there?" Vegas asked, his voice full of concern.

"No, everything is fine. We just need to talk."

"Okay. I'll be there in about twenty minutes. Catch my heart," he said before hanging up.

"I love you," I responded.

When Vegas proposed he said he'd always send his love and it would be up to me to receive it. So each time he said the phrase *catch my heart*, I was sure to respond. It was just a simple reminder of the commitment we'd made. Vegas would say it after arguments, when leaving, when getting off the phone, or anytime he felt I needed a little reminder.

Vegas had been wonderful from the time I announced I was pregnant. He was very attentive to my needs. He would drop everything if I needed something or if I didn't feel well.

Within thirty minutes he was home. We sat down and I grabbed Vegas' hand, looked him in the eyes, and began to explain.

"Vegas, it's very important that you are here for our twins. I'm afraid that with the life you're living there's only two destinations—jail or dead."

Surprisingly, he agreed with everything I was saying.

"I've been thinking the same thing. To be honest, I was actually afraid to mention it to you because I thought you wouldn't agree. I shaped you to be high maintenance, and if we had to budget and couldn't do things like the trips, cars, jewelry and designer wear, I was afraid you wouldn't be happy."

I couldn't believe he thought I was so shallow.

"Baby! I am the happiest woman in the world. There is nothing else I want except security. I want to know that my husband will be home every night."

"Like I've said many times before, I got you and you don't ever have to worry. I always gotchya back. Now catch my heart, girl." I hugged Vegas and gave him a passionate kiss.

After talking for nearly two hours, we agreed he would get out of the game. We came up with a plan to keep our income pretty much the same. Vegas didn't hesitate to agree to the changes. The next step was to make the call to his connect.

"Yo, P. This is Vegas, man. There's gonna be some changes. I'm out the game. I'm passing the baton to my brothers now."

Of course, the connect did everything he could to talk Vegas out of getting out, but there was no use. Next, he called his clients to tell them the same. If they wanted to keep business going, they would now have to go through his brothers. He was passing on the empire.

Over the next couple of weeks, we purchased a few laundromats in the area and began remodeling them. We made them larger, cleaned them up, equipped them with a variety of machines, added a drop-off service, a few TVs, a nice bathroom, a microwave, a number of snack machines and video games. We also allowed 24-hour access. Within a couple of months the laundromats were fully operational. They blew up very fast. We had all types of promotions to boost business. Things turned out better than we'd ever expected.

Life was better than I ever thought possible. I was now four and a half months and already huge. It had been confirmed that I was having girls. I knew it! Vegas and I joined a church not far from our home. We were active members and had begun to arrange for the wedding as well as the twins' christening.

I was counting down the months as they passed. I couldn't wait until that fifth month so that I could start my shopping spree. There was so much to do in so little time. Vegas and I decided I would take leave from work during my pregnancy, so I had a lot of time on my hands to prepare for the twins' arrival. Even though I was no longer working, I was always doing things at the church, keeping everything up to par at the laundromats and constantly doing things around the house. Eventually, I had to slow down because I started to feel not so well. I figured that maybe I was pushing myself too hard. Vegas quickly noticed.

"Why don't you take a break and let me handle things for a while?" he suggested. He would get worried when I started to feel bad. That night, he cooked dinner and we ate in bed. Within a matter of minutes, we were both sound asleep.

Arf, arf, arf . . . Bing, bang, boom!

We woke to the sound of a chaotic terror. Prissy was barking nonstop as we heard noise that sounded like the house was caving in. The huge spotlight that flashed through the bay window blinded me. I didn't know what was going on.

"You trust me, right?" Vegas turned to me and asked.

"Yes," I responded.

"Well, I want you to listen to me and do exactly what I say. You know I would never let anyone hurt you or do anything to hurt you. I want you to lie down, close your eyes, and go back to sleep. When you wake up, everything will be okay."

I trusted Vegas. He never let me down before, so I did just that. I had no intentions of going to sleep until I knew Vegas was safe, but I did close my eyes as he had asked me to do. I began praying to God for our safety as all the commotion went on outside my bedroom doors.

"I love you," Vegas whispered and kissed me. Then, he walked out of the room, closing the door behind him.

I could hear people coming from every direction, stomping up the stairs, slamming doors, and tossing things everywhere. After a few minutes, the house was silent. I walked in the hall and watched as Vegas walked to the foyer with his hands up. He stood still and spread his legs. The men ran toward him and Vegas laid on the ground slowly. This was it . . . the moment I had been dreading our entire relationship. They were there and taking my husband-to-be away from me. I cried silently as I helplessly watched.

"Keep your hands up! Don't move!" A dark, heavy man walked up and cuffed Vegas.

"Laymont Jackson, you have the right to remain silent . . ."

The rest of the words were a blur. I felt faint as I watched the men escort Vegas away. Vegas looked back at me.

"Catch my heart, baby. Catch my heart." His lips motioned as a single tear rolled down his face. The men pulled him and eventually all I could see was the reflection of the letters FBI on the back of the men's jackets.

The next day, I sat by the phone and waited to hear Vegas' voice, but he never called. A day later, he called right after breakfast. He sounded worse than I had ever heard.

"What's up, baby girl?" he said in a low, dismal voice.

I couldn't respond. I just burst into tears. Vegas felt terrible.

"I'm sorry, C. I know I let you down."

"You said you would always take care of me, Vegas," I said forcefully. "You knew this was my worst nightmare and you didn't prevent it from happening." His goal in life was to keep me happy and secure, and he failed.

"I never meant to let you down, Ceazia." I could feel the hurt in Vegas' voice. "I turned my life around. I did everything you asked of me. This was out of my control, baby. I would never do anything to hurt you."

I tried to be strong for him, but I just couldn't.

"What about our twins being without their father and me without a husband? There is no way we can do it on our own."

Like always, Vegas had a plan.

"Baby, I need you to get it together. I need you to stand behind me. Everything will be okay. I need you to go downtown and speak with my lawyer. He'll know exactly what to do."

Vegas was charged with conspiracy to traffic and distribute a controlled substance with Leonardo Figueroa. That was Red's real name. I knew something was up with Red from the day I met him, but I couldn't understand what the authorities had against Vegas. He had been out of the game for months, and he hadn't spoken to Red in even longer.

The next day, I headed for the attorney's office. Once again, I was in the same elevator, pressing the button for the eighth floor. I never would have imagined I would be taking that trip again. As I walked in, I gave the receptionist my name. It was like deja vu.

"My name is Ceazia Devereaux. I have a two o'clock appointment." Right away, I was called to the back. Again, I stood at the door nervously as I avoided eye contact with the handsome, pale man before me.

"Have a seat, Ms. Devereaux," he said invitingly. It seemed like he didn't even recognize me, or at least he acted as if he didn't. He already knew why I was there, so he basically told me the game plan and the price.

"It seems like Mr. Jackson has gotten himself in a little bind. I'm sure it won't be a problem to get a deal for two years in a program. The Feds only have a few photographs of him with another dealer in Mexico and some other places, but no real hard evidence. They didn't recover any drugs or money from the home, and all the money in his accounts traces back to a legitimate source," the attorney explained.

"The only reason Laymont is being held is because narcotics had a big drug bust in Park Place and some of the small fish ratted on the big fish to shorten their time. With the help of those guys, they were able to build a tree of all the dealers in the area. Laymont, along with Red, Bear, and a few other guys, were at the top of the list. After they got all the small fish off the street, they forwarded the information to the Feds so they could get the big fish. You shouldn't worry, though. Laymont will be home in no time," the attorney assured me.

The attorney sounded confident. There was no doubt in my mind things would be okay. I pulled out my checkbook.

"Sounds great. How much will all this cost me, sir?"

"Because this is a federal case, we're looking at ten thousand."

Without any hesitation, I wrote him a check in the amount of ten thousand dollars and left.

As soon as I walked into the house, the phone rang.

"Hello," I answered.

"Hey, baby. What's the deal?" Vegas asked after I accepted the collect call.

"Everything sounds good, baby. Your lawyer says there's no need to worry. At the most, you're looking at a couple of years in a program."

"What?" Vegas said angrily.

"Two years, baby. What's wrong with that?"

"That just won't do, baby. I can't settle for that. Who the fuck is going to be there for you and the girls?"

"We can manage, baby. Things could be worse."

I told Vegas about the bust they had out the way and their intentions to work out deals with the small hustlers so they could get to the big hustlers. Vegas was well aware of the tree. The Feds actually showed him the list when he was in interrogation. He went on to tell me about his experience.

"Yeah, they showed me all that shit during interrogation. They kept asking me about some guy out of Jamaica. They've been following this nigga and his family for years. They were on his ass, but that nigga got smart. The Feds are having problems tracing the money. Without an exchange in money and drugs, there's no way they can pin him. They did seize a ship once, but that led them to a dead end."

As Vegas told me the details of what the Feds had said, my heart froze with fear. *Oh my God! They're talking about India's boyfriend, and if they find out about the money, she'll be on the list as well.* I probed to see how much Vegas knew about the Jamaican kingpin.

"So are you going to work with them, baby?"

"Hell nah, ma. I don't even know this cat. They offered me a deal if I would give him up, but I can't fuck with that. I have too much on the line to become a snitch. And like I said, I don't even know him."

He expressed his worry about the safety of the

twins and me. I told him not to worry and that he would be home soon. He felt a little better but was still upset that he would miss the growth of his twins. He would not be at their birth, and he would not witness their first steps, first tooth or first word. I cried as I thought of not having him with me to share in the milestones of our daughters' first year of life.

Chapter 10
A Lonely Battle

As the months passed, I became depressed and lonely. I turned to the one person who could offer me the support and comfort I needed without being judgmental.

"Hello," my mother answered with her warm voice.

"Mommy, I miss you. I'm so alone and depressed," I whined.

"Awww, baby. Why don't you come and visit me for a couple of weeks?" my mother suggested.

Since I hadn't seen her or my close friend, Chastity, in at least a year, I agreed. My mom moved to Atlanta shortly after her divorce from my father. She felt the move to a new environment was just what she needed for a new beginning. Atlanta was the place for Chastity's new beginning as well. She moved there shortly after her father's death. Hell, if it worked for them, I figured it couldn't hurt me to visit for a couple of weeks, so I happily took my mom up on her offer.

Once I received my call from Vegas and told him of my plans, I quickly packed four weeks worth of clothes, even though I only planned to stay for two. I loaded the Louis Vuitton luggage in the truck and headed for the airport. Two hours later I was in Atlanta.

My mother was at work when I arrived, so Chastity was there waiting for my flight. I was so excited to see her. We had been friends since we were tots. I could see her chatting away on her cell. Her petite frame was outfitted in a power blue business suit, stiletto pumps, with a Gucci clutch bag in hand and Gucci frames. Chastity was about business. Ever since we were young, she knew she would be an entrepreneur. She owned two businesses in the metro area: a strip club and a soul food restaurant. Both of her businesses were of the upscale caliber. She ran her strip club with strict rules. Her girls were top of the line and she took no shit. If they didn't follow her guidelines, they were out the door. Her restaurant served some of the best food in the area. It was a quiet, after work spot with a jazz band.

"Hey, Momma! I can't believe how big you've gotten," Chastity said, hugging me tight.

"I know. It's all stomach, girl," I said as hugged her back.

On the drive to her house, I updated her on all the drama of our friends. In no time, we were pulling up to her house in Buckhead. Her house was beautiful. I was so proud of Chastity's accomplishments. It was hard and she'd had her challenges, but she'd made it.`

A few years prior to Chastity's move to Atlanta,

she was in terrible condition. Her father died, leaving Chastity and her mother to survive on their own. Chastity, like most Virginia Beach girls, grew up with a silver spoon in her mouth. So, when times got hard, she didn't know how to cope with the change. She became angry with her mother and blamed her for their struggle. There were constant arguments between them. Chastity would rebel and her mother would be so hurt. She did not understand what had happened to her sweet daughter. We all tried to reach out to her, but she was just too far gone. It was like she hated the world, so she closed it off. She didn't communicate with anyone or visit anyone. Her entire outlook on the world was negative.

Then one day, she just disappeared. No one heard from her for weeks. After a month passed, she finally contacted her mother. We all were so happy and relieved to know that she was safe. The only information she shared was that she was okay and living in Atlanta. She didn't leave a phone number, address, or any means of contacting her. A year later, she returned to Virginia for a short visit. She was back to the Chastity we all knew and loved. She was confident, optimistic and quite ambitious. She told us of the different projects she was working on. She planned on purchasing a strip club from an associate of hers and she was also looking into either opening a restaurant or a catering business. Obviously, her plan worked, and now she was a successful business owner.

Until this day, we still have no idea what she was doing during those weeks we did not hear from her. In fact, we don't even know what prompted her to just pick up and leave. We suspected it was something illegal. There were even rumors of drug trafficking from Florida to Georgia, but we never had any solid confirmation. We often asked her about her absence and the different rumors, but she just replied with, "I can't tell you, because then I'd have to kill you. Let's just say that it was my secret to an expeditious success!" And we certainly couldn't argue with that, because whatever she did, it certainly worked.

After an hour or so, my mother arrived at Chastity's house. I ran toward her like a small child.

"Mommy! I missed you sooooo much!" She was so beautiful as she walked toward my embrace.

"I've missed you too, honey," she said as she kissed me on my forehead.

I missed her bright smile and glow. My mother is the happiest person I know. No matter what hand she was dealt in life, she would pick herself up, dust herself off, and keep going. Because I had chosen to stay with my mother after the divorce, my dad decided to leave her with everything. That was a wonderful gesture, but the problem was that he left no means of maintaining them. My mother was left to foot the bill for a quarter-million dollar home, three elaborate cars, and my college education. I can remember the times after my parents' divorce when my mother barely had enough money from her nursing salary to pay our mortgage. My mom was forced to stretch her check to maintain the lifestyle that we were so accustomed to.

Luckily, she was not stuck with the responsibility of maintaining my diva status. The weekly deposits my father transferred into my savings account were enough to pay that bill. That was a good thing, too. I couldn't handle the thought of being without those things, even though my mother never even frowned.

"God will provide," she would constantly say as she hummed the tune of *What a Friend We Have in Jesus.* I hated my father for making her suffer the way she did. She worked two jobs just so she could pay the bills and make sure I had the things I needed during college. I never went without, but I was angry that my mom had to work so hard to make sure of that. Her hard work soon came to an end, though. After I graduated from college, my mother felt comfortable enough to move to Atlanta. I, on the other hand, decided I'd made my imprint on Virginia so it was here I must stay. My dad was furious at the idea, but there was no changing my decision. To sway me to change my mind, my dad eventually cut off my weekly deposits. I soon experienced the struggles my mom had once felt, but not even that could change my mind. I was in Virginia and it was here I planned to stay.

My father is the VP of marketing for one of the largest record companies in New York. While in Virginia he held an executive position at a local record company that provided a pretty comfortable living for us. The company eventually merged with a larger company in New York and my dad was the first pick for VP. Because I was still in school, my parents did not want us to relocate right away, so my dad would often travel back and forth between Virginia and New York. This worked great until the time span between the visits began to get longer and longer. It eventually got to the point where we were only seeing him on holidays. My mom suspected foul play. And like every woman, she did her homework to find out. Needless to say, her suspicion was right. My dad was cheating with a young, southern white girl who was working as an intern with the company. He eventually left my mother for this white woman who was half his age.

For a long time, I hated my father. I blamed him for every struggle my mother and I encountered after the divorce. When I think back, he was never a dad. He was so consumed by his job that he never had time for his family. He missed birthdays and even anniversaries. All my mother and I really had was each other, so when he left, I didn't feel alone. Actually, I saw little difference in life at home. There was a financial difference, but that was about it.

Not long after my mother arrived, we decided to head to the mall. Chastity stayed behind, saying she would give us some time alone to catch up.

"I am so excited about my first grandchild!" my mother expressed as we swung into the parking space.

Once we entered the mall, she went wild, wanting to purchase everything. I figured it was okay since I had finally reached my fifth month. She purchased everything from clothes to cribs. She even planned to turn one of her extra bedrooms into a room for the twins.

"I expect to see my grandbabies at least once a month. And when they come, they'll be comfortable in their own little room."

I smiled at my mother's excitement. I was happy to be around someone who shared the excitement of the twins along with Vegas and me.

As the days passed, I started missing Vegas more and more. I cried myself to sleep each night, as I lay alone in my bed. My life seemed so empty without him.

One morning, I decided to take a long, hot bath to relieve some of the pain I was feeling from carrying the twins. I'd been having a lot of discomfort the few days prior. I lit the aromatherapy candles surrounding the bathtub and immersed my body in the water. After five minutes of soaking, I had a sudden urge to urinate. I struggled to lift my 165-pound body out of the tub. I took the first step out, then a watery fluid gushed onto the floor.

"Aaaaahhhhh! Mommyyyyyyyy!!!" I screamed in fear as I stood with my legs apart. She rushed into the bathroom and looked down at the floor.

"Your water has broken, baby. It's a little too early for that, but don't worry," she said calmly as she dialed 911.

My stomach cramped so bad that I gently lowered myself to the bathroom floor and rolled on my side in a fetal position.

"Breathe, baby. Breathe," my mother instructed.

Based on the closeness of my contractions, the 911 operator informed my mother that I was going to deliver soon. I positioned myself on my back and bent my knees. My body shook with pain as sweat rolled from my forehead. With every contraction, it felt natural for me to push. It seemed that was the only way to stop the pain. So, with each contraction I pushed. After several pushes, my first twin was out . . . but there was no cry.

"Mommy! Mommy! Why isn't she crying? Why isn't she crying?" I began to panic. "Please, give her CPR, Mommy. Please, do something to help her breathe," I begged my mother.

It was at that moment the emergency rescue team rushed into the bathroom. They immediately grabbed the first twin, cut the cord and began to deliver the next. Once again, I pushed and the second twin was out. She came into the world with a small, broken cry. Again, the emergency technician snatched the twin away. They hurried us all to the nearest hospital as I bled continuously. When we got to the hospital, I was in terrible condition. I felt like my life was slipping away. I became really cold as everything went black and I fell into a deep sleep.

While sleeping, I dreamt some amazing things. I felt like I was in Paradise as I floated through each image. I vividly remember one particular scene. Children playing in a park surrounded me. I did not recognize any of the children by appearance, but I felt a certain connection with two of the little girls. They were so beautiful. They had caramel skin, long, curly black hair, perfect little teeth, hazel eyes and a beautiful smile to match. As soon as I walked on the playground, they approached me. I could see the little girls were trying to communicate with me, but no words came from their mouths. They pulled me by my arm to an area of the playground where flowers grew. This area was the most peaceful part of the playground. I sat down as the little girls gave me gifts of flowers, teddy bears and drawings. Then, the little girls kissed me on my cheek and pulled at my hand. I tried to get up, but I could not move. The little girls just smiled as they tugged. It was as though they didn't even realize I could not move. In a matter of seconds, the dream was over.

I opened my eyes slowly to the bright lights above my hospital bed. Beside me sat my mother. Her head rested on my leg as she rubbed my hand. She was so excited that I was awake. I could not speak and my body was very stiff. I looked around the room for my twins but they were not there. I wanted to ask where they were, but I could not find the strength for words. As the hours passed, the doctors ran a number of tests and removed many of the tubes that were attached to my body.

The next day, I felt much stronger and was able to speak. The only thing I wanted was to see my twins. Again, my mother was right beside me when I woke.

"Mom, how are my twins and where are they?" I asked.

I had a heavy feeling in my heart as I awaited the answer. By the look on her face, I knew it couldn't be good.

"I'm sorry, honey. Your twins didn't make it. I already contacted the prison so they could relay the news to Vegas. I'm so sorry, honey," she said in a broken voice.

She explained to me that I had been in a coma

for the past month. She went on to tell me the events that followed the delivery of my babies.

"After giving birth to the twins, your uterus didn't contract, so you kept bleeding. You lost so much blood that you became unconscious and eventually comatose. Once they got the babies and you to the hospital, they rushed you into surgery.

The entire time you were in a coma, your twins struggled for their little lives. They were less than two pounds each and very underdeveloped. One struggled with lung problems while the other struggled with fluid on her brain."

I cried as my mother told me the ups and downs of their struggles. They were holding on for dear life and their mommy wasn't even there to comfort them and help them during their fight. I felt so bad. My mom said the girls fought until I came out of my coma, at which time they died simultaneously. I was crushed as I imagined my daughters' struggle. I didn't understand what I did to deserve such pain. I thought maybe that was the ultimate punishment for all the bad things Vegas and I had done. I prayed for an answer.

God, we turned our lives around and attended church each Sunday. I gave continuous praise and worship for all my blessings. I just don't understand why You would allow something so terrible to happen.

A week later, I was discharged from the hospital.

"Honey, I think it's best you stay with me a little while longer. You seem a little depressed," my mom suggested.

I agreed to stay with her a couple weeks longer. During that time, I constantly questioned the Lord.

"If all things of the Lord are good, then why does He allow tragedy?" I would ask my mother.

My mother answered each question with a spiritual response.

The Lord does not allow anything to happen in vain. He allows us to go through things to bring us closer to him."

Sad to say, I was not happy with the "God works in mysterious ways" or "it's just a test of faith" or "the Lord has a plan for you" responses. I really didn't want to hear the name God or Lord, period. I felt like God had played a cruel trick on me, and I definitely didn't find it funny. At that point, the Lord and I were on opposing teams.

My mother sensed my anger and felt there was only one way to save me from my despair.

"Why don't you come to church with me this week? We're having a healing convocation. I think it may help you feel better," my mother suggested.

I refused with no explanation and shut myself off to all things. I just wanted to return home.

Chapter 11
Divas Need Therapy Too

By the time fall rolled around, I was back to wearing a size three. The laundromats were doing great and Vegas was doing well, too. I traveled to Richmond each weekend to visit him. He had been sentenced to one year. The federal charge was dismissed, but he had to serve one year of his probation for being out of the state when we were in Cancun. He estimated he would only have to serve about ten months.

My body recovered well after my surgery, but emotionally, I was still in pretty bad shape. I decided to visit Charlotte in order to cope with the anger I was feeling over the twins' death. Our meetings were productive. Each week, she would give me a task to work on. One particular week she instructed me to take notes of the times when I was happy and not feeling frustrated at all. Before she gave me that task, I felt that I had little to no frustration, but once she gave me the task, my life became hell.

On the way from the session, a police officer pulled me over for a fake ass violation, but I knew my only real crime was driving a nice car in the Great Neck area of Virginia Beach while young, black, and beautiful. When the prick walked to the car, he didn't ask for a registration or license, but instead ordered me to step out of the car and put my hands on the hood. Of course, I refused.

"What exactly are you pulling me over for, sir? Would it be racial profiling, by chance?"

He got very angry at my refusal and sarcastic response and proceeded to pull me out of the car. Once he got me out, he held one arm behind my back and grabbed my neck with his free hand. Then he forced my face on the burning hood of the car and put the cuffs on me. Needless to say, I did not pass go, but went straight to jail with no "get out of jail free" card. He claimed he was pulling me over because my car fit the description of a stolen vehicle. However, I didn't fit the description of the suspect.

As soon as I was released on a personal release bond, I called my attorney, then, I contacted Asia. Asia was the bitch of all bitches when it came to things like this. As a bank executive, Asia rubbed elbows with all sorts of powerful people. There wasn't an issue she couldn't solve. She told me not to worry; she would take care of things. I didn't worry, because I knew that with my attorney and Asia's connections, plus her "super bitch" attitude, the devil would run for cover.

* * *

It seemed like that incident was the beginning to an eternal hell. The few days after that were even worse. After working out one afternoon, I came home to a yellow bag from the Sheriff's Department. I was not happy seeing that damn bag on my gate. I snatched the bag off and began to read: *Virginia Beach Juvenile and Domestic Court In reference to Karen White versus Laymont Jackson.*

Now I was pissed.

What in the hell does he have a subpoena for, and who the hell is Karen White? I thought.

I couldn't wait to get his call. I was prepared to fry his ass. *He's already put me through enough shit and now this,* I thought as I walked to the front door. It wasn't long before I received the call that I had been anticipating. As soon as he said 'hello', I let him have it.

"What are you talking about, C? I never even heard of a Karen White!" he pleaded, but I wasn't buying it.

How could he not know her when she's got our address, his name, and his date of birth?

I felt like I was going to have a nervous breakdown. I screamed and slammed the phone down. I walked back and forth and let out a crazed cry. I was acting so crazy that Prissy ran under the bed and hid during my tantrum. I had to do something to calm down, so I made myself a drink. I made a Belvedere and orange juice, turned on *No Letting Go* by Wayne Wonder, sat in the Jacuzzi, and smoked some hydro. I was blazed as I sang with Wayne:

Got someboooooody,
Sheeee's a beauty,

Very speeeeeecial,
Really and truuuuuuuuly.
Takes good care of me,
Like it's her duuuuuty.
Walk riiiight by my side,
Niiight and daaaaay.

The truth in those words was amazing. The girl he spoke of in that song was me. I did all those things for Vegas and he deceived me. I went against everything that my parents taught me for the love of Vegas, and he stabbed me in the back. That brought so much pain to my heart that I just sat and cried. A little while later, I found myself a little tipsy and decided to get some rest.

I awoke to the sound of the intercom.

"Ceazia . . . Ceazia."

It was Asia and she was at the gate. I buzzed the gate open and met her at the door. Asia stopped by to give me an update on everything she had done.

"I contacted the officer's superior and filed a complaint for you. I also contacted the Mayor's office and a local newscaster. I notified the NAACP and a local chapter of civil rights activists. Once we finish with his ass, he's gonna be willing to turn in his badge. I'm thinking you should even pursue a civil suit."

That's why I loved Asia so much. She was definitely a doer and not a talker. She was on a mission to make the officer's life a living hell and her mission was just about complete. As we were talking, the phone rang.

"Hello."

"Hey girl, I need to talk to you." It was India.

"I swear you twins have some psychic connection. Asia just came over."

"Well, tell her to leave. We really need to talk," India demanded.

I told Asia I would speak to her later since her sister was having a crisis. Asia left and I went back to the phone.

India was so upset. She told me about a very disturbing call she received from her fiancé's brother.

"Samuel has been apprehended by the Jamaican police. They tied him to a number of murders and it doesn't look good. Samuel has been set up by someone, but we have no idea who. He knew it had to be someone close, and from the way his brother speaks, I'm a suspect," India said, crying uncontrollably as she told me the story.

We all knew what that meant. Whoever Samuel felt had the slightest possibility of being the snitch was surely on death row. He would kill every possible witness before he would serve time. We were surprised he didn't have a shootout with the police when they arrested him. Normally, all types of soldiers, ready for war, would have been surrounding him, but this time the authorities caught him alone. His brother didn't exactly say what Samuel was doing at the time he was apprehended, but the evidence pointed toward sex.

India didn't know what to think. Not only was her man in jail, he was cheating when he was arrested, and he might even have someone try to kill her. She wished that she had listened to me when I used to tell her about all the wicked things involved in that life. We had to do something, not only for her safety but also for her sanity. Our plan was to find out who set up Samuel and to find out if he really was cheating. The most important thing was to keep India alive while we were doing our research. She decided she would stay at my old condo and take leave from work until things got a little safer.

The following weekend, I went to my next counseling session with Charlotte. When I walked in, she noticed I had not improved at all.

"Oh my, Ceazia, you look terrible. Why didn't you call for an emergency session?"

I cried as I told her all the events of the week. I didn't understand how so many terrible things could happen to one person. I just wondered what was in store for the next week.

"Well, let's see how we did on the assignment. Tell me a time when you felt relaxed," she said.

"Sadly, the only time during the entire week that I was truly relaxed was after a ten minute session with my dildo," I responded, truly embarrassed.

I would have told her about the time I sat in the Jacuzzi and drank Belvedere as I listened to reggae and smoked a blunt, but I didn't think that would draw a pretty self-portrait. I would be classified as a drunk and druggie on top of having to discuss how I used artificial things to give me false happiness. As we talked, she gave me a number of exercises to do when I found myself most stressed. They included breathing exercises, meditation, and muscle stretches. I thought it would be much easier if she would just prescribe Prozac, but at this point, I was willing to try anything, so I agreed.

Due to a call from my father, as soon as I got home, I had the opportunity to try the stress relief exercise Charlotte taught me.

"I would like you to come to New York for Thanksgiving," he said. And like every call, we ended up arguing.

"No way. I refuse to spend Thanksgiving with you and your dumb blonde wife. Besides, since you cut off my weekly deposits a long time ago. I can't afford a trip to New York," I lied in an attempt to make my father feel guilty.

"Anyway, I'm sure you'll be busy working, so what's the point?" I continued my guilt trip.

He was so persistent that finally I just agreed to go and hung up the phone. Once I hung up, I did the exercise. I started with my toes and tightened each muscle then relaxed it. I did each muscle until I reached my neck. Amazingly, it worked. I actually felt relieved after I did the exercise.

That night, I called the girls and we decided to have dinner. We went to one of our favorite spots, a local soul food joint in downtown Norfolk. I was happy. It had been a long time since all of us were able to get together in one centralized location. With the exception of India and me, everyone seemed pretty happy.

Tionna was excited to tell us about her new man, Jonathan. He was the gynecologist who'd examined her at the health department. We all found that very funny. She told us how she ran into him a month later at the grocery store. He approached her and actually asked her out, and they had been dating ever since. She told us that they even talked about adopting Tonya's baby. They decided that since Tionna could not have children, they would adopt the little boy. They did not have a decision from the adoption agency yet, but they were confident that everything would go through. We all were happy that things were finally going well for Tionna.

After we ate, we decided to go sit near the stage and listen to the poetry. As we listened, I noticed India kept looking over her shoulder.

"What are you doing?" I asked her, annoyed at her constant motion.

She pointed to a tall, slender, dark girl who sat at the bar. The girl was dressed plainly and wore a turban. India said the girl had been looking in our direction for the past thirty minutes. I assumed she was just being paranoid, so I ordered her a Long Island Iced Tea to calm her nerves.

That dinner was just the atmosphere I needed. For the first time in a long time, I felt relieved. There was no stress at all. We all laughed, joked, and drank for the next hour. When it was time to go, we were all pretty toasted. I decided to follow India to make sure she got home safely since she was the most drunk. The condo was on the way to the Interstate, so it was on my route home. As she was pulling off toward the complex, I saw her make a sudden stop. I stopped behind her and headed toward the car door. As I approached, she opened the door and stuck her head out. Two seconds later, vomit was everywhere. Just the smell of it made my stomach turn, so I quickly turned and headed back to my car.

"Pull into the garage," I yelled.

I followed her and helped her into the condo. When we got inside, I filled the tub with aromatherapy bath pearls and warm water. I helped her undress and placed her inside the bathtub. While she was bathing, I went to the kitchen to make some cappuccino.

All of a sudden, I heard a loud thump. I figured she had probably fallen, so I headed to the bathroom to make sure she was okay. On the way, I felt a draft coming from the direction of the living room. When I reached the living room, I noticed the French doors were cracked open. I opened the doors completely to inspect and there was India standing on the balcony, butt naked and dripping wet, pointing a gold glock with a pearl handle to her head. She had no idea I was standing right behind her.

She sobbed as she prayed in a soft whisper. "Lord, forgive me for the ultimate sin which I am about to commit..."

Bam!

At that moment, we both spun around at the sound of the French doors shutting. A tall, slender frame stood before us. In the person's hand was a long, silver machete that glistened in the dim light. Instinctively, I jumped on the person and pushed the lanky body against the rail of the balcony. As we struggled, the towering person pushed the machete toward my neck. I became weaker and weaker as the struggle progressed. The dark being didn't seem to lose any strength, and the machete was pressing against my neck. It took every ounce of energy in my body to keep the force from cutting my throat. I could feel the pain as the knife began to slice the skin and the blood slowly trickled down my chest.

Bang . . . bang . . . bang . . . bang!

And the struggle was over. The dark beast fell to the ground, stiff and lifeless. The balcony and doors were covered with dark wetness. I turned around to see India standing motionless with the gun pointing straight ahead. Smoke rose from the barrel as she stood in the dark.

Chapter 12
Wonderful Closures

Things slowly came together as the months passed. I attended court with Vegas for the case he had in Virginia Beach Juvenile Domestic Court.

"Karen White versus Laymont Jackson" the court clerk announced.

As I walked in, I noticed a much older woman with a child who looked at least twelve years old. *Now I know Vegas was a male whore in his younger days, but this is ridiculous. In fact, it's virtually impossible,* I thought as they brought Vegas from the back holding cell and stood him in front of the judge. Then the judge explained that they were there for child support. Vegas looked back at me pitifully and I glared at him with a look of death. While the judge spoke, the woman looked at Vegas as if she was in a state of confusion.

"This is not my child's father. I'm here to collect back child support from Laymont Jackson," the woman said after the judge finished speaking.

"That is Laymont Jackson," the judge responded.

As it turned out, the courts had subpoenaed the wrong Laymont Jackson. Vegas was telling the truth. He didn't know that woman after all. I felt so bad that I had doubted him. I should have trusted him. I watched as the deputy took him away in shackles. He looked at me and gave me that same mesmerizing smile from the first day we met and whispered, "Catch my heart."

Tears rolled from my eyes as I blew him a kiss and mouthed the words "I love you."

For the first time in months, I felt like I loved Vegas and missed him. I had so much anger and frustration inside of me over the past few months that I nearly forgot what it was like to love.

Things with India were continuously progressing. She returned to work, and with Charlotte's help, she got over Samuel as well. After the shooting at the condo, everything came together. The masked person from that night was a female by the name of Chantelli. She was one of Samuel's soldiers. It was the same girl India had seen in the restaurant that night. We slipped up when we went to our favorite restaurant. Samuel knew India would end up there eventually so he had the girl stake out the place for weeks until we showed up.

We soon found out that Samuel's brother was the culprit behind all the hysteria. He was jealous of Samuel's success, so he set him up. He knew if Samuel was killed or jailed, the empire would be passed on to him. Therefore, he contacted the authorities and gave them leads on a number of murders. Then, he gave them the cue for the arrest. Because he was Samuel's brother, he knew there were only a few instances when Samuel would be alone. Usually Samuel was surrounded by his soldiers and they were always ready for war. However, his brother knew Samuel had one thing he did alone, and that was sex. So, when Samuel was in the act, his brother gave the signal. The police rushed in and caught him with his pants down, literally. He was standing ass naked, with penis strong, getting what seemed to be the head of a lifetime.

We were surprised to learn a bootie boy was giving the head he was receiving. Who would have ever thought the don dada would be getting sucked off by a homo? That's why he was alone. He was so afraid of someone finding out about his secret life that he would risk his safety and send his soldiers away. Any good kingpin would have known that would be his downfall.

India was infuriated by Samuel's infidelity. She wanted to get even. She wanted him to pay dearly for breaking her heart. She had put her career and her life in danger by doing the money exchange for him. She was even going to leave the States, move to Jamaica, and marry Samuel. And to think the entire time he had a secret life. He had to pay.

India asked that I lay an evil cloud above his head for the misery and pain she suffered. The evil spells of voodoo were not something I usually practiced, but I agreed. The smell of cinnamon was in the air as I did the wicked trickery. The empire of his family would surely fall and his soul along with it.

Tionna and Jonathan decided to get married. They were planning a huge wedding at the botanical gardens in Norfolk. Tionna arranged for a wedding party of at least fifteen and invited five hundred guests. They would spend their honeymoon in Paris. I was so happy for Tionna. She deserved Jonathan, the wedding, and the honeymoon. She was dealt bad hands her whole life, and it was finally her turn to be blessed.

Although they were not granted the right to adopt Tonya's little boy, she was still happy. The adoption agency felt the circumstances by which the child was conceived did not make Tionna the best candidate for the adoption. They did grant the adoption to her uncle, though. We were just happy the child was going to be raised by a family member. Tionna and Jonathan had plans of their own to have a child. With Jonathan being a gynecologist, he did plenty of research on a number of studies about infertility. He arranged for Tionna to try infertility pills, injections, and if neither of those methods worked, in vitro fertilization.

Once they got married, they were planning to move to Atlanta. Jonathan landed a job with the Centers for Disease Control and Tionna wanted a new start. Her life was finally on the path we all dreamed of and we wished her well.

* * *

As the days passed, I continued missing Vegas more and more. Each weekend I would travel one hundred miles to visit him. I hated the constant struggle with the deputies every weekend. First, all the visitors lined up to be sniffed by a dog. Then, the butch female deputies sexually harassed us. Each week one particular female deputy would give me a hard time. I don't know what it was about me, but she just did not like me.

I wouldn't be surprised if she was fucking Vegas, I would think to myself each weekend.

One visit she had the audacity to say, "Excuse me, ma'am. Do you have a thong on?"

I looked at her with a cold stare and said, "No, I do not."

In fact, I had no panties on at all. It took all I had to keep from smacking the color off her face.

After the harassment session, we were seated on hard folding chairs as we waited for our loved ones to come out. Even though I went through hell to see Vegas, I enjoyed each visit.

I was always dressed for easy access. Vegas had it worked out with the correctional officers to simply ignore us when we went into the broom closet during each visit. The closet was about the size of a bathroom—just the right size for a quickie. Vegas would unfold the chair that was conveniently placed in the closet, pull down his pants, and sit with his penis at attention. That was my cue to pull up my skirt and hop right on it. I would ride him until he released inside me. It was amazing all the positions we could do in that chair. Vegas' favorite position was when I would sit on his penis facing away from him, grab my ankles, and bounce up and down. He loved to see my ass bounce while he watched his penis disappear deep inside my vagina. After our quick session, our visit was over and I was on the road home.

I would immediately run to the car to retrieve the wet wipes and panties that I had waiting. I would clean myself up, put on the fresh pair of panties, and hit the road. After a few visits, I was used to the drive and made it home with no problem.

Chapter 13
Reach for the Rasta

Thanksgiving finally rolled around and it was time for me to take that dreaded trip to New York to see my father. The flight was smooth and I figured it would probably be the highlight of my entire trip. I knew hell was waiting. When I arrived at the airport, old blondie herself was waiting.

"Hel-lo," I greeted sarcastically.

Before she could even return the greeting, the drama began.

"Darling, you look terrible. Was your flight here okay?"

Now what type of shit is that to say? What if I thought I looked great?

"Yeah, the flight was kind of rough, so what's your excuse?" I glared at her. Even though the flight was fine, I needed a comeback.

During the entire drive to the house, she quizzed me.

"How are things back home? Did that boyfriend of yours get out of prison yet? How is your mother?

Is she still caring for sick poor people at that city hospital?"

A look of disgust crossed my face as she blabbed on and on. When she finally took a breath, I got my chance to fire back.

"Life at home is great. The business is doing well, and Vegas will be home soon. And as far as my mother is concerned, that's none of your business. Now, if you would like to know how things were before you became my father's mistress, I can certainly tell you about that."

I would never tell that wench anything she could use to belittle me. She did everything she could to make me look bad and make herself look good. That's the only way she could lift herself up, because in reality, she was nothing without my dad.

It was cold and windy as I walked to the front door of my father's house. The butler met me and quickly took my coat. The house was warm and I could smell the aroma of fresh brewed coffee. I was shown to "my quarters" as the balding butler said in an English accent. The room was huge but not very welcoming. I don't know who my dad used as his interior decorator, but from the looks of things, I'm sure the dumb blonde had a lot to do with it. I felt like I was walking into a barn. The theme of the room was antique country, and it was disgusting. I felt like singing old Mac Donald as I entered. There was definitely a moo-moo here and a quack-quack there. There were farm animals everywhere—the wallpaper border, linens, and even the pictures on the wall.

Once I was settled, I decided to give Carmin a

call. She was in New York preparing for a Thanksgiving fashion show for the stars. I was glad she was close by to provide me relief from the Addam's family.

"Carmin's Creations," she said as she answered the phone.

"Hey girl! Where's the party at tonight?" I said, surprising her.

"Ceazia Devereaux! What the hell is going on?" Carmin excitedly responded "You know the fashion show is on Thanksgiving, so I'm gonna be really busy. But I'll pick you up and we'll go to the show and then the after party. I have someone I want you to meet."

Carmin knew damn well I wasn't trying to meet nobody.

Don't nobody want to meet no possessive ass 'I want you and my girl plus my man's girl' type nigga," I complained.

"I'll be there at eight. Dress to impress," Carmin said, ignoring my statement.

"A'ight girl," I simply said, and with that, we hung up.

Just then, the butler knocked at the door. "The man of the house would like you in his presence."

"And where might that man's presence be?" I laughed and said in a mocking voice.

He directed me down a long hall to my father's study. My father sat behind a huge maple wood desk in a burgundy leather chair reading a newspaper. When I entered, he looked over his glasses.

"Hi, darling. How are you?" he asked.

He seemed happy to see me, but I'll never know if it was genuine. My father had changed so much.

He acted like he had a stick up his ass. He was such a stiff. When he lived with my mother and me, he didn't speak the way he does now, he didn't dress the way he does now, and he definitely didn't have the same taste in women. Who said money doesn't change people?

I gave my father a big hug. I really did miss him, even though he did so much to hurt me. I told him about everything that was going on at home. He was really bothered that his baby girl was surrounded by such drama. He gave me a long lecture on how I should move to New York so that I could be closer to him and he could protect me.

If I'm gonna end up anything like you, I definitely don't want to move, I thought.

The next day, I woke up to breakfast in bed. The maid knocked on my door.

"Breakfast, Ms. Devereaux."

I looked over at the clock and it read seven a.m.

"Come in," I said, still half asleep.

The maid walked in with a tray that consisted of breakfast, a newspaper, and a carnation. It instantly brought back memories of Cancun.

"Thank you," I said as she turned to leave. I barely touched the food as I cried. I thought of the wonderful times Vegas and I had in Mexico and how much I missed him. It had been four months since Vegas was locked up and I felt so alone.

Ring, ring . . . ring, ring.

"Who in the hell is calling me so early? I looked at the caller ID on my cell phone. "Carmin. What the hell does she want so early in the morning?" I grumbled. "Hello."

"C, wake up."

"I am awake, and what do you want so early?" I said as I plucked the crust from my eyes.

"I'm headed to a video shoot and I want you to meet the artist. I'm on my way to get you now. Get dressed!"

Knowing that putting up an argument would be useless, I dragged myself out of bed and got dressed. Thirty minutes later, Carmin was out front and honking her horn. It didn't take long for us to arrive at the location of the shoot. It was just as I imagined: cameras, half-dressed chicks, make-up artists, and lots of wannabes.

"There's Cobra," Carmin said as she grabbed my arm and pulled me along.

"What up, Carm? Who's that you got with you?" The dark, bald guy asked in a deep, scratchy voice. I really wasn't interested in entertaining this guy or his entourage, but I spoke up for Carmin's sake.

"I'm Ceazia, but you can call me C."

"Okay. Nice to meet you, C."

As he was speaking, I noticed one of his boys who stood apart from everyone else. He seemed to be in a deep phone conversation, but he was constantly giving me the eye. I pretended not to notice and walked over to the refreshment table for bottled water. That was the only escape from Cobra. Carmin walked over soon after me.

"So what do you think, girl?"

"I think I'm not interested. But his boy, the one with the dreads, Lakers throwback, and baby blue Pradas . . . he can get it," I responded.

"Damn, girl, you were watching him like that?"

"Don't front, Carmin. You know how we do. It doesn't take but five seconds to do a complete rundown and calculation of net worth, deductions already included!"

"Okaaaaayyyyy!" we both shouted in our best sistah girl voices as we gave each other a high-five.

The video shoot was long and tiring. I could have sworn they shot each scene at least ten times. It lasted until ten at night. Afterwards, we all decided to meet at Club Inferno at midnight. The limo brought us right to the front and we walked in. The club was jumping! People were packed shoulder to shoulder as we squeezed our way to the VIP section. We sat amongst Cobra and his crew. I made it my business to sit as close as possible to the dread-wearing brotha from earlier. The waitress brought over bottles of Cristal back to back. That's when he finally spoke.

"Ya want a drink, gal?"

Oh my goodness! He has an accent! I think I'm in love.

"Aye, do ya 'ear me, gal? Ya want a drink?"

I was so mesmerized I forgot to respond.

"Yes, I do. I would like a screwdriver," I said in my most seductive voice as I gave him the eye. It was as if he didn't even notice as he ordered the drink for me.

"I don't know what his problem is, but I am the hottest chick in here," I whispered to Carmin. "He can't front but for so long. I will have him by the end of the night."

As the night went on, I did everything I could to get his attention without making it too obvious.

I bent over the table to speak to Carmin so that my breasts would be clearly visible. I crossed my legs so that the split in my dress would show thigh up to my hip, and I even started small talk with him first. Nevertheless, he still seemed unmoved. I was finally fed up with this Rasta, so I decided to go find Carmin. In no time, I found her at the bar talking with a few Spanish girls. I noticed one girl staring at me, so I decided to break in the conversation and get Carmin's attention.

"Excuse me. Carmin, I need to speak to you for a second."

"Hey, girl! Let me introduce you to my girls. Everyone this is my girl, Ceazia. C, this is Maritza, Chloe, Lachele, and Arizelli."

Arizelli, Arizelli. Why does that sound familiar? I wondered as I looked at the girl and tried to put a face with the name. She smiled at me seductively. My confusion must have been obvious, because Carmin began shaking my shoulder and shouting.

"C . . . C . . . You all right? What the hell you been drinking, girl?"

That's when it hit me. *Cancun . . . Arizelli. I know it's a small world, but how the hell did this happen?*

"Hellooooo . . . Ceazia?" Carmin was still trying to get my attention.

"Oh, I'm sorry, girl. My head is just spinning. I think it's from mixing those drinks. I just came over to tell you I'm giving up on the Rasta. For some reason, he's just not feeling me."

"What? Nah, there has got to be something up. I'll be over there in a minute. You need to sit down and sober up a little."

As I walked away, I noticed Carmin grabbing Arizelli around the waist as they whispered in each other's ears.

I returned to a seat far from Donovan, the Rasta. I made it a point not to notice him or acknowledge his presence at all. Then, just as the night was starting to get boring, the DJ began to play reggae and the party was on.

"Come down, selecta!" I heard a voice yell.

It was Donovan, and he was once again turning me on. Each time the DJ played a rhythm the crowd liked, Donovan would throw his fingers up and yell, "Buk, buk, buk, buk," while banging his Guinness bottle against the table.

I was feeling nice and having a ball. When the DJ played Sean Paul's "Gimme the Light," I jumped to my feet and started to win'. Everyone stared as I moved to the West Indian tunes. Out of nowhere, someone came behind me and began to dance along. I turned around and smiled when I realized it was Donovan.

"Ya dance like a yahd gal," he whispered in my ear.

I did it. I finally did it. If I had known all I had to do was win', he would have been mine a long time ago, I thought as I continued to dance even more seductively.

"Thanks, but no yardie taught me these moves," I said as I walked out of my win' and into the steps of Spragga Benz. Dancing was my drop, so if that's what he wanted, then that's what I was giving. I did every dance move I could think of. By the end of the night, he was eating out of the palm of my hand.

"Dancehall princess, come 'ere. I want ta speak wit' ya," he said as I took a break to sip on my drink. I sat beside him.

"Dancehall princess?" I questioned.

"True. Ya move de crowd. It's like a wicked spell."

"Oh, that's what it is?" I responded sarcastically.

"I not know the trickery of ya Creole gal. You wind up me heart with that evil art."

Listening to Donovan was like interpreting Shakespeare, but I did well with my interpretations.

"Are you insinuating I used voodoo to put you in a trance through my dancing?"

"Ya, mon. I notice at first glance ya to be wed, so I stand clear. But now, like a magnet, you're near."

I don't know if it was the drinks or what, but the more he talked, the more he sounded like a reggae song. I had to clear my head, so I excused myself.

"I'm sorry, but I'm feeling a little sick. I'm going to get a bottled water."

"Take dis, keep da change."

I walked away and headed back to the bar. As I got closer, I could see Carmin still chatting with Arizelli. She kissed her on her lips and began to walk in my direction.

Oh my goodness, Carmin is gay! What do I do? Does she know I just saw that? I don't know if I'm ready to have this conversation with Carmin. But before I could decide what to do, Carmin and I were face to face.

"Hey, girl. I thought you were going to come back over to VIP with me earlier," I said nervously.

"Well, reggae came on, so I knew you would be fine. How long have you been standing here?"

"Not long. I mean, I just started walking this way."

"Ceazia," Carmin said as if she knew I was lying, "follow me. I need to introduce you to someone." We headed back toward the bar with the same girls.

"Okay, Carm, I think you had too much to drink now. Ummmm, you introduced me to all these girls earlier," I said.

"I know, but I really need to explain some things about one girl in particular."

Once we reached the bar, she grabbed Arizelli by the hand and we all went back to the VIP section. To my surprise, Cobra and his crew all knew Arizelli. This was getting weirder by the minute. We all sat down and Carmin began to explain.

"Ceazia, Arizelli is more than just a friend to me. She is my lover."

"Lover? As in you-are-gay lover? Or you're just-curious-so-let's-try-this lover?" I asked.

"I'm not gay, C. Nor am I just curious. I love Arizelli and I am bisexual," Carmin said with confidence.

Now, how am I supposed to tell Carmin that not only me, but me and Vegas both, had sex with her lover? I pinched myself to see if I could wake from this nightmare. *Damn, I'm not dreaming. I'm awake.*

"C, what's wrong? Do you have a problem with my sexuality?"

I guess I was thinking a little too long.

"Nah, girl. Do you? You're my girl. I'm going to

love you regardless of your sexuality. But just explain why."

"C, I could no longer continue being second. No matter how hard I tried or what I did, I was never going to be number one in my previous relationship. When Arizelli came along, I was number one. She loved me unconditionally, and she gives me all the attention and affection I could ever want or need."

I reached over and hugged her. As we hugged, Arizelli licked her lips and blew me a kiss.

"It's cool, Carm. I love you, girl."

"Thanks, C. I love you, too. Let's keep this just between us for now. Okay?"

"Okay."

A while later, the club began to clear out, so we said our good-byes and went our separate ways.

Chapter 14
Thanksgiving with the Addams Family

"Rise and shine," the maid said as she knocked on the door. Again, I was greeted with breakfast in bed. I ate the fruit as I thought about the previous night.

Carmin is lovers with Cancun Arizelli. Wait until I tell Vegas. Even worse, I think Arzelli still wants me. Or maybe she wants Vegas because she never really got a taste of the dick. Do I tell Carmin or not? If I tell Carmin, then my secret is out, but if I don't, then it's like I'm betraying her. How did I get myself in this one?

"Knock, knock."

"Yes."

"Good morning, honey. Can I come in?"

"Sure, Dad. Come on in."

My dad came in and sat at the end of the bed. "We have a long day today. I want to start the day off with church service. Then, we'll eat about three. How does that sound?"

"That's fine, Daddy. I promised Carmin I would go to the Thanksgiving celebrity fashion show with her tonight, though," I explained to my dad.

"Hey, I have tickets to that. Maybe your mother and I will go too."

"That's stepmother, and I think I'd rather go with Carmin."

With nothing left to say, my dad left and began to prepare for church.

Church service was long and boring. It was nothing like the down-home Baptist services that I was used to. I couldn't believe this woman changed everything about my dad, from his attire to his religion.

Dinner was served shortly after we returned from church. The table setting was beautiful. The room was dim, with candles lighting the table. There was enough food to feed a village in Africa for at least a month. At the table were my father and I, the wicked witch, and a few of her family members. My dad and I were outnumbered even in his own home. A pianist played classical music as we ate dinner and the butlers stood at each end of the table waiting to move on command. I found this all quite humorous.

"Darling, what is so funny?" the gold digger asked.

"Nothing. I was just thinking to myself."

"Why don't you tell the family about your little business you run in Virginia?" Like always, she was trying to make me look like I was nothing.

"If you are referring to the chain of laundromats I own, I will be more than happy to share," I responded.

I told them all about how we started with only one facility that we remodeled and how in a matter of months we nearly owned one in each of the seven cities. The family seemed rather interested in my success. When I finished my story, blondie's mother stepped in.

"Oh my, that is a wonderful success story. I love to hear about underprivileged black kids who grow up and make something of themselves, like you and your father."

My father must have seen the steam rise from my head because he quickly intervened. "Mother, you are out of line. My child has never been poor."

That's it! All of them have pissed me off now! Dad was only offended by the suggestion that I was poor? What about the generalization of black people? I thought as I tried my best to bite my tongue. Only five seconds passed, but I could no longer do it. I had to respond.

"I have had it with all of you! Dad, you are a poor excuse for a strong black man. You're the reason our black youth have no male role models. And to the wife and mother blondie, neither of you have ever accomplished anything in life. It's like you were raised to seek men who are well off so you can sit on your uneducated, Southern belle asses. I'm out of here. Dad, you can have your so-called *family!*"

I stormed to my room and immediately called Carmin. *The nerve of those people,* I thought as I dialed Carmin's number.

"Hello."

"Carmin, it's C. Come get me, girl."

"Okay. What's wrong?"

I told her all about the dinner conversation as I pulled out something to wear. I needed something cute yet funky, so I pulled out my black Manolo Blahniks, tight-fitting fatigue pants, and a black shirt designed by Carmin. The shirt emphasized my breasts and showed plenty of back and stomach. I made sure I pulled the drawstrings on the pants just above the top of the boot, and I threw on just the right accessories to complement the soldier theme.

"Ceazia!" My dad shouted as he stood at the bedroom door.

"I don't want to talk. Leave me alone."

He entered the room anyway. He tried hopelessly to explain away the incident that had occurred during dinner. I ignored his weak excuses for his so-called family and continued to prepare for the night. My dad noticed my inattentiveness and became quite agitated.

"Do you hear me talking to you?" he asked angrily.

I could no longer take it. I had to tell my dad how I truly felt. I'd been holding my tongue for years and it was finally time to let go.

"Yes, father. I do hear you. I hear all the tired excuses you're giving for your family, for your actions, and for their actions. Well, I'm really not interested in any excuses. I'd rather know your reason for leaving me and mom. Or your reason for leaving me to fight on my own after college. You're quick to tell me that Vegas is not the guy for me, but he's the one that's been there for me for the last couple years. He's been doing all the things that you used to do. I don't know what happened dad, but you've truly changed and I really wish I could have my daddy back." Those were my last words before grabbing my coat and heading toward the door.

My father did not respond. He just sat in disbelief with his head down. I guess he'd never taken the time to examine the effect the divorce had on me.

Carmin was out front in no time. I jumped in her truck and we headed for the plaza where the fashion show was being held. It was chaotic getting to the front row seat Carmin had reserved for me. I sat amongst Cobra and his crew once again. I was disappointed that Donovan was nowhere to be found.

"What up, C?" Cobra asked as he looked up and down my body.

"Chilling. What about you?" I sat one seat away from him. I refused to be right underneath his annoying ass.

The music blasted as the first model walked out. Carmin had really outdone herself this time. The outfits the models wore were the shit! I was so into the show I didn't even notice someone had taken the seat next to me.

"Whattem," I heard a pleasing voice in my ear.

"Donovan. What's up, baby?"

"Ya save da seat 'ere for me, gal?" he asked as he licked his sexy lips. Just his presence was making me moist.

"Not exactly, but if you would like to sit here, that's fine."

We continued to watch the show as the crowd went wild. In no time, the show was over and I headed to the back to meet Carmin. On the way, I stopped by the concession stand to purchase a dozen roses.

"You did great, girl!" I rushed over, gave her a hug, and handed her the roses. I had no idea Carmin was doing such great things with her career.

"Thanks, girl. I put a lot into this show. So you really enjoyed it?"

"Sure did," a voice said before I could respond. To my surprise, it was Arizelli.

"Hi, baby," Carmin said, excited to see her bisexual mate. They greeted each other with a small kiss.

"What up, Carm? That shit was hot!" Cobra said as he walked over with his entourage. I was really beginning to get irritated when Donovan caught my eye. I gave him my most seductive glance then turned to Carmin and finished our conversation. I was sure to give him just enough attention to turn him on, but not so much that I looked desperate.

It worked. He's on his way over, I thought as Donovan walked toward me.

"Whattem," he said in a sexy accent.

"Hey, Donovan. What's the deal?"

"Not much. You goin' to the dancehall tonight?"

"I think so. I'll have to see what Carm is doing."

"Hope ta see ya dere," he said as he walked away.

Just as I expected, we headed to Club Inferno after the show. This time the club was twice as packed as the night before.

"Hello, ladies. Right this way," the bouncer said

as he unhooked the velvet rope so that Carmin, Arizelli, and I could enter.

"I'm a hustler, baby. I just want you to know, it ain't where I been, but where I'm 'bout to go." We all sang to the tunes of Jay Z. Pharrell was really blowing up and putting VA on the map, so Carmin and I had to represent.

"Aaaahhhh . . . you can tell when they playing some old VA shit," Cobra said as we walked over to the VIP section.

"Don't hate, nigga. Maybe if you have Pharrell drop some of that VA shit on your tracks, you'll go platinum," I said playfully. We all laughed as we sat to order some drinks.

"I'll be right back. Nature calls." Carmin excused herself to the restroom. Not thirty seconds had passed before Arizelli was moving her hand up my thigh. I grabbed her hand tightly and whispered through my teeth, "I don't know what you're trying to prove, but I'm gonna let you know up front ain't nothing jumpin'."

"In due time, baby . . . in due time. Carmin said the same thing at first, now look at her," Arizelli whispered back while grinning. Then she licked my earlobe.

I can't believe this bitch. She has some nerve, I thought as I tried to keep my composure. It took all I had to keep from smacking the shit out of her. I immediately got up. I could no longer take it. I had to tell Carmin what was going on. I didn't care how she would respond. I had to tell her. I hadn't taken two steps before I was knocked off my feet. People were running frantically as I heard the gunshots ring out over my head.

Pop . . . pop . . . pop . . . pop . . . pop!

The shots seemed never ending. I crawled under a nearby table to keep from being trampled. I sobbed softly as I waited for the chance to escape to safety.

"Come wit' me," I heard Donovan say as I was lifted into the air. I didn't say a word as he carried me out through the side door. Outside the door, people were screaming, crying, bleeding, and searching for their loved ones. All the mass hysteria reminded me of 9-11. We rushed over to Donovan's car and jumped in.

"I have to find Carmin," I said as I began to panic.

"No fear, princess. She wit' de man."

I assumed 'de man' was Cobra. I decided to try calling her cell. The phone rang constantly, but there was no answer.

"Can you call Cobra? Carm isn't answering her phone and I want to make sure she's okay."

Donovan called and got the same response; no answer. Now I really began to worry.

"Dere is much commotion. Dem can't 'ear dem phone."

Donovan did all he could to relax me. "Come wit me to dem hotel. Dem a go be dere shortly," he suggested.

For some reason, I felt safe with Donovan, so I agreed to go back to his hotel with him. Once we got to the hotel, the valet came out and parked the car. It was not until that moment that I realized the model of car Donovan was driving. I could have fainted.

Oh, my fucking stars! This nigga drives a Mercedes CL6.

Again, my face must have been screaming my thoughts because Donovan gave me a devilish grin as he said, "Me princess like de car, aye?"

"It's nice," I replied, trying not to seem too impressed.

Before heading to the room, we stopped in the hotel restaurant to grab a little to eat. We called Cobra and Carm's phones constantly. Eventually, my phone went dead.

"Can we go to your room so I can use your phone?" I asked. I was beginning to get tired, but couldn't even think of sleeping until I was sure that Carmin was okay.

Upon entering his room, I immediately plugged my phone into the charger that I had luckily placed in my purse before leaving home. Then, I called Carmin's phone again. This time her voicemail came on immediately. I didn't know what to think. We couldn't reach anyone. Cobra and Carm's phones must have both been dead.

Why didn't they call anyone? Wouldn't Carm want to know I'm okay?

All sorts of thoughts ran through my head. We tried calling Cobra's room, but there was no answer. Donovan even hit him on the two-way. Still there was no response.

"Why doncha take a hot bath? Relax ya'self," Donovan suggested. Before doing so, I left a message on every phone. As he filled the tub with hot water and bubbles, Donovan called some of the other guys from their crew to see if anyone knew anything. He left the bathroom to give me some privacy while he continued to make some calls.

Once the bath was ready, I jumped in and

turned on the tub jets for a more calming effect. It felt like a load was lifted off my shoulders as I soaked. Donovan brought in a glass of champagne for me to sip as I relaxed. The only information he could get was that a female was shot. No one knew who she was or her condition, but they did say they saw Carmin and Cobra leaving the club during all the commotion. After hearing that, I was able to relax. In a matter of seconds, I was asleep.

Ring, ring . . . Ring, ring . . . Ring, ring.

I woke to the sound of the phone. My head was spinning as I sat up to answer.

"Hello," I answered in a cracked voice.

"C?" It was Carmin.

"Carmin! Where are you?" Her voice sounded weak and sad. I could feel something was wrong.

"I'm at Manhattan Hospital. I need you to come here right away," she said.

"What's wrong? Where's Cobra? Didn't you get my messages? Are you alright?" A thousand questions ran through my head as I spit them out at her.

"C! Please, just get here. I need you now, C."

I immediately hung up the phone and jumped up. My body ached all over as I struggled to get out of the bed. Underneath the terry cloth robe, I was naked. I couldn't remember how it happened, but I really didn't have the time to figure it out. I just assumed I must have fallen asleep in the tub and Donovan put me to bed.

"Donovan, wake up!" I shook him as he lay on the couch.

"Whattem?" he responded sleepily.

"We got to hurry. Something's wrong with Carmin. She's at Manhattan Hospital. She sounded really upset."

We quickly hit the streets. We made it to the hospital in ten minutes. As soon as I walked through the sliding doors, I saw Carmin. Cobra was holding her as she cried uncontrollably.

"Nooooo!" She was screaming. Her body was trembling with pain. I walked over to her and she hugged me tight. "C! Why, C? Why?" She spoke the words forcefully.

"Why what, honey? What's going on?" I asked in a tone of motherly love.

"I can't live without her! I just can't."

That's when it hit me.

Oh shit! Arizelli! Something has happened to Arizelli.

"Is it Arizelli, Carm? What's wrong with her?"

"She's gone, C. She's gone."

At that time, I had a full understanding. There was no need to say anything else. We just hugged as she cried.

Chapter 15
A Lover's Triangle—
Who's to Blame?

When I returned home from New York, I had a continuous discomfort in my vagina. I thought it may be a yeast infection, but Monistat just wasn't giving me any relief. So, I called and made an emergency appointment with my gynecologist. When I walked in the busy office, I was seen right away.

"Right this way, Ms. Devereaux; exam room four. Get undressed from the waist down, please. The doctor will be right in," the nurse ordered me.

I quickly got undressed and the doctor came in soon after. The exam was horrible. It was the worst feeling. I was glad when it was over.

"It looks like you have gonorrhea," the doctor said as if it was second nature to say such things.

"I don't think that's possible, doctor. I'm in a monogamous relationship."

"I'm most certain it's gonorrhea, Ms. Devereaux."

Okay, maybe this bitch doesn't understand. I thought as I tried to reiterate.

"As I said before, you can't be right. *In fact,* I was recently examined and there was no trace of an STD," I lied.

"Well, maybe you don't recall when it happened and I am unable to pinpoint it, but either way, you have gonorrhea and it needs to be treated. You're more than welcome to have a second opinion if you prefer. Would you like to have an HIV test as well, ma'am?"

The nerve of this bitch! "No thank you," I said as I jumped off the table and snatched the prescription out of her hand. "What I would like is to get dressed now," I said as I glared at her. She attempted to explain the course of treatment but I quickly interrupted her and again requested she leave so I could get dressed. This time she left without hesitation.

How in the hell did this happen? I asked myself this question repeatedly on the way home. I thought of every possible scenario. *Maybe I got it the night I was at the club with no panties on. Maybe it was something in the bed at my dad's house, or maybe it was the hotel bed, tub, or robe.*

Still, I knew that none of these could have been the cause. I had to have had sex with an infected person in order to get an STD. In the back of my mind, there was a possibility that was just too real. I just didn't want to face it.

Maybe it's from Vegas. Maybe he really is screwing that deputy. Or even worse, I could have been raped.

Yeah, that's it. It had to be Donovan. Vegas would never do such a thing.

My cell phone rang as I was driving. It was Donovan and I was quite pissed at him because of the realization that I'd come to face.

"What?" I yelled into the phone.

"Why de princess raise 'er voice so?"

"Fuck you, Donovan. I know what you did. You filthy, nasty, walking STD!"

"Whattem? Why you so angry?"

I burst into tears as I envisioned how it happened.

"You . . . you raped me! You preyed on me when I was weak. You put something in my drink when I was in the tub. That's why I couldn't remember how I ended up with the robe on. That's why I had such a headache, and that's why my body ached so badly the next morning. You raped me! I hate you and I hope you die!"

"De princess fall asleep in da tub and me take you out and wrap you in dat dere robe. Me even sleep on de couch and leave de bed for da princess." Donovan sounded sincere as he explained, but the suspicion was still there.

"Liar! You fucking liar! I hate you! Don't ever call me again!" I slammed the phone shut as I cried.

The days were cold as December rolled in, so the girls and I decided to go on a little winter shopping spree. We hit every mall in the area. We started at Lynnhaven and ended at Patrick Henry, hitting every one in between. Since we had been together all day, we decided to go to the club later that night. We all rushed home to get dressed. The plan was to meet at the club around midnight.

I decided to wear one of my new outfits. I laid out my khaki cargo pants with the drawstring, my burgundy Gucci pumps with legwarmers, and a burgundy sweater that hung off one shoulder. I wore my hair in one ponytail to the right with huge, gold bamboo earrings and a tan Kangol hat. I looked in the mirror once I was fully dressed.

I laughed to myself as I looked at my gear. Just like *Flashdance*.

Ring, ring . . . Ring, ring.

"Hello."

"Whattem, princess."

Why in the hell is he calling me from a local number? I wondered as I snapped on him.

"What do you want? I asked you to stop calling. What don't you understand about I hate you and I hope you die?"

"Me came to get de princess back," Donovan said persistently.

"Look, Donovan, I was never your girl, gal, or 'de princess'. So I would really appreciate it if you would leave me the hell alone. Okay?"

Click. I hung up in his ear.

Ring, ring . . . Ring, ring.

Oh no, this muthafucker is not calling back!

"Hello!" I screamed at the top of my lungs.

"Why the hell are you yelling, C?" It was Tionna.

"Oh sorry, girl, I thought you were someone else."

"Whatever. I'm ready, so come get me," Tionna demanded.

"And who the hell said I was picking you up?"

"No one. It's understood. I'll be waiting. Blow when you're out front."

"Good-bye," I said before hanging up. Five minutes later, I was at Tionna's house, and she ran right out.

"What's up, bitch?" she said as she jumped in. She turned up Sean Paul to blast as we headed to reggae night at Club Cabana. The parking lot was full when we arrived. That was of no concern to me since I would be utilizing the VIP parking.

"What's up, Mrs. Vegas? Pull right in there," the dark, heavyset bouncer said, pointing to a parking spot right in front of the club. I could tell by the familiar rides that all of Vegas' boys were in the club.

Good thing I kept it classy tonight, I thought as I parked the car. Vegas' boys were sure to tell if I had on my 'fuck'em girl' dress.

We walked right in as the other girls stood in line shivering. Once inside, we headed straight to the bathroom where we met Mickie, Carmin, India and Asia. They were all touching up their hair and makeup. Once we finished the final touches, we headed out of the bathroom.

"Yo, C! What up, baby?" Vegas' older brother yelled.

"Hey, Snake. What's been up?"

"Same shit. You all right? You need anything?" he asked. Since Vegas' brothers had taken over the empire, things were lovely for them.

"I'm fine. Thanks for asking."

"Well, at least let me buy you and your girls a drink," Snake pleaded.

"Hell, yeah! I'll take a margarita. That's what I'm talking 'bout."

All my girls jumped at the opportunity for a free drink, shouting out their drink orders.

"Well, I see everyone is in agreement, so let's head to the bar," Snake said as he slithered over there.

"Girl, he is fine. Hook a sistah up," Mickie whispered in my ear as we trotted to the bar in a single file line like a group of kindergartners.

"Girl, we don't call him Snake for nothing," I quickly responded, trying to give her fair warning.

"Pssshhhh . . . Nothing I can't handle."

"Mickie, his name describes him perfectly. He is as slick as a snake. He charms women so well that they're blind to his venom. I've even heard stories of him screwing his girl, then while his girl slept, he went downstairs to screw her sister. If that's not the moves of a snake, I don't know what is."

"Well, I'll be the first to break him. Are you gonna put me on or not?" Mickie pressed, still not shaken by my speech.

"Okay. Don't say I didn't warn you."

I walked over to Snake as he was handing out the drinks.

"My girl, Mickie, wants to know what's up with you."

"Oh yeah? Where she at?" he asked as he scanned all my friends with his shifty little eyes.

"She's the one with the big breasts, wearing red."

He quickly spotted her and landed his eyes on her breasts as she walked forward.

"Daaammmnnn, baby. You're wearing that dress," Snake said as he handed Mickie her drink.

"Oh, you like this?" she asked in her most seductive tone. Just looking at them made me sick.

"Alright, y'all, I'm out. Do your thang."

The other girls hit the dance floor. I stood near the floor as I sipped my drink. I refused to walk on the floor and be called out by the DJ.

"No drinks on the dance floor," the DJ was constantly yelling. I would laugh as I saw the culprits trying to play it off and dance their way off the floor.

"Whattem, princess?" I heard Donovan's voice as he squeezed my arm. *What the fuck is he doing here in VA?* I wondered.

"Donovan, you're hurting me. Please let me go."

"Come wit' me," he demanded as he pulled on my arm.

"Okay. Just let me go. I don't want to make a scene."

We both headed out of the club. I tried to make eye contact with Mickie and Snake as I was leaving the club, but they didn't even notice. I could see Snake fondling Mickie with his hand up her dress. Just as I was hitting the door, Martinez was entering.

Thank God. With his big ass mouth, he'll be sure to tell Snake I left the club. He was my only savior, so I had to get his attention.

"Martinez!" I yelled as I was leaving.

"What up, baby girl? You out already?" he asked, looking back and forth between Donovan and me.

"Yeah, the girls are in there, though. I don't feel well. I just need some fresh air."

"A'ight. Holla back, mami," he said as he shrugged his shoulders and walked inside the club.

The cold winter air hit my body as I walked toward my car.

"Why you a act so angry to me?" Donovan asked.

"I know what you did, Donovan, and I hate you for it, so please just leave me the fuck alone."

Donovan's eyes became fiery with anger as he grabbed me by my throat.

"What da blood clot? You nah go nowhere, muddaskunk."

Tears rolled down my face. I spoke to him calmly as I unlocked the Mace on my key chain.

"Please, Donovan, let me go. We can work this out," I pleaded before pressing the trigger on my Mace.

"Aaaaaauuuuuuuuuuugh! Bitch!" Donovan screamed as I emptied the can in his face.

"I hate you, and for the last time, I hope you die, you Rasta bastard. Now who's the muddaskunk?"

I jumped in my car and skidded off. I had never been so afraid in my life. I never thought I would need that Mace, but it had certainly come in handy.

The next morning, Vegas called bright and early. "How you doing, baby?" he asked in a strange voice.

"I'm fine, boo. How are you?"

"I'm good. How was the club last night?"

I knew the word would get to him pretty quickly since all his boys were there.

"It was alright. Don't worry, baby. I represented well."

"Oh, I'm not worried about that. Anybody fuck with you? Any disrespect?"

Should I tell him or not? He may already know and is just testing me. I had to think quickly.

"Why you ask that?"

"C, answer me. Did anyone fuck with you?" His voice was starting to get edgy. I knew Vegas was vexed, and there was no time for playing. I had to come with the truth.

"Yeah, baby. But I took care of it."

"What you mean you took care of it? Is this nigga still breathing?" Vegas was clearly not happy with my response.

"Of course. You know I didn't kill him."

"My point exactly. So, you ain't take care of shit. Next time, don't let me have to ask you when some shit like that go down. That needs to be the first thing out your mouth. Now stay the fuck out of sight for a while."

Click! Vegas hung up in my ear.

Why is he so mad? Who told him and what did they say?

Things were definitely getting out of hand.

The next few days were quiet. I was surprised I hadn't received any harassing calls from Donovan. Just as Vegas requested, I stayed out of sight. His brothers were handling things for me at the laundromats while I enjoyed the relaxation. Each day I would practice my shadow boxing then relax in the Jacuzzi. My nights were spent reading in front of the fireplace or watching a movie in the theater room. This was the first time I actually had a chance to enjoy the amenities of our home.

"C! Open the damn gate. It's cold as shit out here," Mickie yelled through the intercom. I buzzed her in.

"Giiiirrrrlllllll, that Snake is something else," she said as she handed me the stack of newspapers that were collecting at my gate. I began to go through them as she rambled on.

"He sexed me so good last night."

Umph, must run in the family, I thought as I reminisced about all the times Vegas made sweet love to me.

"Girl, I think I'm whipped. He kissed and caressed every inch of my body. He took his time and pleased me in every way. It was like he was truly in love with me. It felt like we were making love. My pussy is getting wet just thinking about it."

"Oh my God!" I yelled as I dropped the paper.

"What girl?" What's wrong?"

I couldn't speak. I just covered my mouth. My heart was pounding profusely.

"Ceazia, what the hell is going on, girl? Talk to me," Meikell said as she tried to shake some sense into me.

I picked up the paper and read the headline aloud, "Body Found Hanging from Chesapeake Bay Bridge."

"West Indian native identified as Donovan Daniels was brutally murdered," I continued. "The body was found missing arms, and the genitals were also removed. This is one of the most brutal murders in this area in the past decade."

Mickie had no knowledge of the incident between Donovan and me, and I was glad that I hadn't shared our escapade with anyone.

"That's Carmin's friend, right?" Mickie had no idea.

"Yeah, girl. It's crazy how you can be here one day and gone the next," I responded.

"I know. Well, on that note, I think I better run and try to get some more of Snake's dick, because who knows when it may be my time to go."

"Mickie! That's a horrible thing to say."

"Whatever, girl. I'm out." She gave me a big hug and left. I watched as she jumped into her car and pulled out of the driveway. Mickie still had her promiscuous ways, but she had certainly come a long way.

Ring, ring . . . Ring, ring.

The caller ID read Carmin Sorano.

"Hey, Carm."

"Did you read the paper?" she asked, agitated.

"Yeah, isn't that sad?"

"Sad?" Carmin was confused by my response. "This is terrible. You don't even seem worried."

"Why should I be worried?" I asked. I thought that maybe Carmin was insinuating the Jamaican Mafia would be after me or something.

"C, how much of the article did you read?"

Now Carmin was starting to scare me.

"I read the part about his death. Did I miss something?"

"Obviously, Ceazia. You're wanted."

"What?" I could feel the tears beginning to well up in my eyes.

"If you had read the whole thing you'd know it

says he was last seen in front of a local nightclub with you. They described you from head to toe and even your car. They have a witness saying they heard you telling him you hated him and that he was going to die. You're the lead suspect. What are you going to do, girl?"

"I didn't do it. Carm, you know I'm not capable of doing such a thing. How did I get myself into this? I have to go."

I hung up the phone and began to pace back and forth. *What in the hell is going on? What did Vegas do? I can't go to jail, Lord.*

The words "Lord, help me" almost escaped my lips, but I quickly remembered the evil trick he played on me by taking my twins. Their death was still heavy on my heart and I had not been to church since. *He's not in my corner. No need to call on Him.*

As time crept by, I contemplated what I should do. I knew I didn't have much time before the detectives would show up at my front door asking questions, or worse, taking me into custody. I thought about calling my mother, but I didn't want to worry her. Vegas was my only hope.

Why the fuck isn't Vegas calling? I wondered as I watched the seconds tick on the grandfather clock. Not able to wait any longer, I got dressed and headed to the state penitentiary.

"Visit for Laymont Jackson!" the butch looking female yelled. Once Vegas entered the visiting room, I walked right up to him, firing questions.

"What the hell is going on, Vegas? I'm wanted for murder. I don't know what to do. I can't—"

Vegas put his finger to my mouth.

"Shhhhhh," he said, hushing me up. He took my hand and led me to the broom closet. Inside, he started to kiss me passionately. My heart began to beat uncontrollably.

Oh shit, we can't have sex. I may still be infected with gonorrhea. I haven't finished the antibiotics yet. What in the hell am I going to do? As a distraction, I began to cry.

"Sit down and listen to me. You don't need to worry. Go ahead and speak with them. You didn't do it, so you know nothing," Vegas said, trying to offer comfort.

"But what if they don't believe me, Vegas?"

"Baby, didn't I say I will always protect you?"

"Yes."

"Well then, listen to me and do as I say."

Vegas opened the door and kissed me on the lips before walking away.

"Catch my heart," he said before walking through the prison door and back to his life behind the prison walls.

"I love you," I responded before leaving.

That visit was really odd, I thought as headed out the door and toward my car.

"Bye," the deputy said with a smirk on her face. That was also odd, because normally that same bitch would have been giving me a harder time. Now more than ever I considered the possibility that her and Vegas were fucking. It was just too much of a coincidence. Vegas did not push me to have sex, he cut the visit short, and then that bitch says goodbye to me on my way out.

Maybe Vegas did give me gonorrhea, I began to think. *If Vegas gave me gonorrhea, then that would mean that Donovan was innocent. That would also mean that he was killed for no reason. It's all my fault. If I would have never accused him of raping me he would have never come to Virginia and he would still be alive. What have I done?*

I cried the entire way home as I thought about the terrible mistake I might have made.

As I approached the house, I could see police cars surrounding the block. I knew exactly why they were there. They had finally caught up with me. I was so exhausted and drained at this point that I didn't even run. Besides, where would I run? I had been struggling for the past few years and was finally tired of fighting, so just as Vegas did the night of his arrest, I surrendered peacefully. I stepped out of the car, hands in the air and legs spread apart. The officers quickly ran over and patted me down. Then, they quickly placed the cuffs on me as they read me my rights. Once they explained that I had been charged with the murder of Donovan Daniels, I was placed in a car and rushed off to the police station.

Once we reached the station I was immediately placed in an interrogation room. The process was long and draining. The detectives asked me the same questions repeatedly.

"Where were you on the night of the murder of Donovan Daniels? How did you know Donovan Daniels? How long were you acquainted with Donovan Daniels? How were you all acquainted?"

They went on and on, question after question. They knew someone else must have been involved, so they offered me numerous plea bargains if I would reveal that person. Unfortunately, I hon-

estly didn't have any information I could share
with them. The detectives had evidence they
wouldn't reveal that indicated I was not the actual
killer, so they reduced my charge to accessory to
murder. Because I didn't give them the name of
the actual killer, they thought I was trying to protect someone, and that's how I was stuck with no
bond. My hearing followed shortly after my arrest.
Things were going downhill fast.

Chapter 16

What Happened to "I'll Always Protect You"?

The court was silent as the twelve men and women walked in and seated themselves. I looked at my girls and gave a sigh.

This is it, I thought as the reality sunk in. It had been two long weeks of court sessions but it only took two hours for deliberation.

"Please stand for the verdict," the judge said in a cold voice. The bailiff brought over a small piece of paper that held my destiny.

"We the people find Ceazia Devereaux guilty as an accessory to the murder of Donovan Daniels," the judge read aloud. "Sentencing is as follows," he continued. "Ten years, two of which will be served in the state penitentiary, then released into the state's women's recovery program for the remainder of the sentence."

Bam! The judged banged his gavel.

"Court is adjourned," were the final words I

heard before the judge rose from his chair and exited the courtroom. The deputy walked over and slapped the handcuffs on my wrists. I ached with pain as the metal squeezed against my bones. I looked back at all my family and friends who had come to support me.

"Noooooo, don't take my baby! Nooooooo!" my mother screamed hysterically.

Her cry sent a piercing pain to my heart. I was all she had and now I was being taken away from her. The guilt I felt was almost unbearable. My father grabbed her as she collapsed to the ground. I couldn't take it any longer. I stopped and looked at her.

"I'm sorry, Momma . . . I'm sorry," I spoke as tears rolled from my eyes.

Who's protecting me now? Where is Vegas? I thought he would always protect me, I kept asking myself over and over again as I was escorted from the courtroom.

The Virginia State Penitentiary for Women was no place for a prissy little Virginia Beach girl like myself, and they made sure I was aware of it. Everyone hated me, from the deputies to the inmates. I had to stand my ground and make a name for myself, and I did just that. It's just unfortunate that it was a deputy who had to feel the pain of my pent up aggressions.

As I was in line getting breakfast, a deputy approached me.

"Identity yourself, inmate!" she yelled in my ear, demanding I read off my inmate number. Unfortunately, memorizing a six-digit identification number was not a priority of mine, so I didn't know it.

"My name is Devereaux . . . Ceazia Devereaux," I responded, avoiding eye contact.

"Identify yourself, inmate!" she yelled again.

At that point, I knew she was not going to leave me alone until I gave her the response she wanted. Therefore, to make her happy, I decided to look at my wristband and read the number off to her. Just as I lifted my wrist to read the numbers, she hit my arm with her baton. Without thinking, I jumped in her face.

"What the fuck are you thinking, bitch?"

That's when I recognized who she was. It was the deputy from the penitentiary where Vegas was being held.

"Sooo, I finally got a response out of you?" she said with a mischievous grin.

"Look, I don't know what it is you have against me, but I don't want any problems," I tried explaining. Unfortunately, she wasn't trying to hear it.

"Yeah, once I heard Vegas' little princess was an inmate here, I put in a request to pay you a little visit. I intend on making your stay here a living hell."

The more and more she spoke, the more and more that bitch was pissing me off, but I tried to remain calm.

"Okay, deputy. May I continue to get my breakfast now?" I responded, trying to end the conversation. I figured being passive was my best approach to the situation.

"Sure, you may leave, but before you go, think I oughtta tell you something."

"And that is?"

"Vegas likes it when I bounce on his dick while he sits in the chair too. Now catch *my* heart, bitch."

I didn't give her a chance to say anything more. Again, I reacted on impulse.

Smack!

I lifted my tray and hit her across her face. I completely blacked out as I continued to hit her over and over and over again with the metal tray. Other deputies and correctional officers rushed over within seconds. They grabbed me and dragged me straight to solitary confinement.

The cell was lonely and cold. I sat in my new home, depressed.

Vegas did have sex with her. He actually fucked her. I repeated those words in my head. I never thought the day would come when Vegas would cheat on me. I always thought he loved me with all his heart. Now I knew he was the one who had given me gonorrhea. It was because of his deceit and lies that Donovan was dead and I was in prison.

The more I sat alone in that cell, the more the realization set in. There was no longer a phone, cable TV, Hypnotic Poison perfume, or even Prissy curled up beside me in bed. For days, I sat without food or water, hoping that I would die without anyone even noticing. The New Year was two days away and I planned to pass into a new life just as midnight rolled in. I figured that seven days of forced starvation would put me right at the dying point. I also had a suicide drink that one of the inmates slipped me, just in case.

I spent half an hour writing a letter to my loved ones as the final hours before midnight quickly approached.

To all I love and adore,

I have reached a point in my life that I am no longer a pleasure to you all, but a problem. When one thinks of me, it's no longer love, but instead it's sadness. Sadness that I am away, disappointment for the actions I've been accused of, and anger for such a sudden separation. I sat and wondered what I have done to deserve such a punishment. It's as though I have a curse upon my life. So, I've decided to free us all of the misery and lay down for an eternal rest. I love each and every one of you.

I didn't even bother to sign the bottom. There were five minutes left until midnight and I could feel the energy leaving my body. In five minutes, I would drink the suicide concoction. I decided to pray. Even though I was tired of life, I still wanted to be welcomed in the gates of Heaven.

God, I ask for Your forgiveness as I leave this place. I ask that You have mercy on my soul and allow me to enter the eternal gates of Heaven. I can no longer live the curse I am living each day. I was torn from my children, I have been falsely accused, and I am alone, Lord. This is the bed I have made and I am prepared to sleep. If You are truly present, please help me.

I held the drink and prepared to take my final breath. Suddenly, my body became numb. I tried to lift my arms to swallow the suicide drink, but I was unable to move. Tears began to roll down my face.

Boom . . . boom . . . boom!

I could faintly hear the sound of fireworks outside my window. I opened my eyes and watched from my cell window. From a distance I watched. I knew that people were dancing, yelling, and hugging in the city streets afar. It was now 2003 and I was still here. I was still alive by the will of God. Vegas did not protect me, my mother did not protect me, and not even my friends could protect me. My body was physically restrained, but my spirit was now free.

"Thank you, Father, for rescuing me," I whispered softly as I shredded my suicide letter.

Chapter 17
Welcome Home

*C*ling . . . *click, click, click, click* . . . *bam!*
The sound of the gate closed behind him.

"See you soon, Jackson!" the deputy yelled through the gate.

"Fuck you, deputy. You'll never see me in this bitch again," Vegas responded as he walked toward his brother, who was waiting in the car. It had been ten long months and Vegas was happy to finally be released.

"What's up, nigga?" Snake said as he hugged his younger brother.

"Happy to be home, man. Happy to be home," Vegas responded. Yes, he was happy to be home, but he knew he would still be alone without me around.

"We got some shit planned for you, man. I'm gonna take you to the crib and let you get situated. We'll be there to pick you up around noon."

Snake had the whole day planned for Vegas. He was going to make sure his little brother came home with a boom. Vegas had other things on his mind, though.

I gotta get my girl home. I gotta make some power moves and fast, he thought as they pulled up to the house. Vegas was surprised to see the house just as he left it. He had expected his brothers to destroy it.

I see everything is still intact here. You guys even kept up the landscaping and maintenance," Vegas said, surprised at how well his brothers had kept the house.

"Yeah, man. We weren't trying to hear your fucking mouth," Snake joked. Vegas jumped out of the car and headed to the house.

"I'll be back about twelve, man, so be ready," Snake yelled out the window as he pulled off.

Arf . . . arf . . . arf!

Vegas could hear Prissy barking as he put his key in the door.

"They even took good care of you, Prissy," he said as he patted her on the head. Once inside, Vegas headed straight for the shower. When he entered our room, he paused. The full size portrait of me really saddened him.

"I'm sorry, C. I'm sorry. I was supposed to be there to protect you. Nothing was ever supposed to happen to you. I love you, baby, and I'm gonna get you home," he spoke aloud as he adored the portrait.

He hopped in the shower to wash away all the memories of his imprisonment. Vegas exited the shower ready for a new beginning. He turned toward the closet, disappointed that he would have to wear an outdated outfit.

Damn, I'm not trying to wear no old ass shit. If my baby was here, I know she would have all the latest shit here waiting for me, he thought.

"Daaaammmmn!!!" Vegas yelled as he opened the closet door. His brothers had looked out for him big time. His closet was stocked with all the new Tims in every style and color, all the newest throwbacks, Prada sneakers, Evisu jeans, team jackets and even a few packs of fresh, white tees. They got him everything he could possibly need, including socks, boxers, toothbrush, his favorite toothpaste, deodorant, and lotion. All of his jewelry was freshly cleaned and buffed. Vegas felt on top of the world as he got dressed. After dressing he decided to check out the rest of the house. Everything was exactly as he remembered. Nothing had changed. Vegas then decided to make a few calls since he still had some time to waste.

"Hello," a female voice answered.

"What's up, yo?"

"Who is this?" the female responded rudely.

"Come on, I don't have time for the games. Where my kids at?" Vegas asked.

"What kids? Oh, we've found another baby daddy," she said before hanging up in Vegas' ear. Before he could pick up the phone to dial again, the phone rang.

"Hello."

"You have a collect call from—" the recording began to say. Vegas immediately accepted the charges.

"Hey, baby!" I said, excited to hear his voice. It had been so long since we'd spoken to each other.

Vegas had no idea the deputy spilled the beans about his infidelity. I decided not to bring it up. I had other plans for that. I kept in mind what Vegas taught me in the beginning of our relationship: Sometimes you just have to let shit ride and keep your enemies close.

"How are you, C? Everything okay? Are they treating you right in there?" Vegas asked a thousand questions at once.

"I'm fine, baby, considering my state."

"Well, I'm gonna do everything I can to get you out of there. First thing tomorrow, I'm gonna holla at my lawyer about getting you an early release. Okay?"

I didn't get my hopes up because I didn't think much could be done. On the other hand, I didn't want to discourage Vegas.

"Okay, baby. Do what you can." I'm sure Vegas felt responsible for getting me locked up, but in reality, he should have. He lied to me, causing me to act irrationally. As much as I loved Vegas, the deceit remained in my head.

"Alright, baby. Call me tomorrow. I love you, baby girl."

"I love you, too," I said before the call was disconnected.

Ring, ring . . . Ring, ring.

"Hello," Vegas answered again.

"Yo, nigga, come the fuck outside. You ready to roll?" It was Snake.

"A'ight, nigga," Vegas said before hanging up. When Vegas opened the door, his other brother and Martinez were there to greet him with a bottle of Belvedere.

"What's up, nigga?" they both yelled before bombarding him with masculine hugs.

"I hope you ready, nigga, because this is about to be a three-day party," Martinez said as they got in the car. Each one of them handed Vegas a thousand dollars in cash as a welcome home gift.

"Thanks, niggas. That's the least y'all mutha-fuckers could do since y'all been living in my shit rent free." They all laughed.

"I see you like the gear, too," Martinez added.

"Whatever. Y'all niggas did a'ight." They continued to laugh as they made the first stop of the day, which was the barbershop.

Vegas got a fresh cut with a sharp edge-up. By the time they left the barbershop, they had finished the bottle of Belvedere, so they headed to the liquor store to replenish their stock. They purchased a bottle of Hennessy and more Belvedere. That would be enough to last them for the next few hours.

After a day of visiting and catching up, it was time for the welcome home bash. Martinez and Snake arranged for the party to be held at the local strip club. They had one section of the club reserved for his guests only. They had all types of food trays, including wings, seafood, cheeses, fruits, vegetables, and other heavy finger foods. The section was decorated with a welcome home banner and a huge throne awaited the king of the night.

"Welcome home!" everyone cheered as Vegas entered the club. Strippers were coming at him from all directions. The females were more excited about the party than he was. As soon as he sat in the chair, the party began. Snake and Martinez had paid the dancers in advance to give Vegas the show of a lifetime. They did everything except sex each other in front of everyone. The club was chaotic that night. It was full of drinking and hormones. That was surely a welcome home night to remember.

Chapter 18
Bring Home My Baby

After all the welcome home partying, it was time for Vegas to begin his mission to rescue me. Early Monday morning, he went to see his lawyer.

"Mr. Jackson, glad to see you," the lawyer said as he extended his hand. "Back so soon?" he questioned as he directed Vegas to be seated.

"It's not me this time, man. It's my girl. You handled her murder case for me. Her name is Ceazia Devereaux," Vegas explained.

"Oh yes, Ms. Devereaux. That was a tough case. What can I do for you?" the lawyer asked.

"Well, I was hoping for a reconsideration on her time. She has no priors and I think we can get her released into a program or probation or something. I just need to get her out of there."

"I understand, Mr. Jackson, but without the actual killer behind bars, it's hard to get her off. She's going to have to work with the detectives on this one. Murder cases aren't my specialty, but the

Commonwealth attorney and detectives were willing to work something out if she would give them some leads. Unfortunately, she was not budging. You think you can get her to work with us?" the lawyer proposed to Vegas.

"She really doesn't know anything, man. She told you all she knew. Is there anything else I can do?" Vegas pleaded with the lawyer.

"I really don't think so, Mr. Jackson, but I'll speak to the Commonwealth and see. How has her stay been so far? Any disciplinary actions?"

Vegas was hesitant to answer, but he knew he had to be truthful.

"Well, she started off on the wrong foot. She was sent to solitary confinement for assaulting a deputy, but that is currently under review because the deputy provoked Ceazia."

"Okay, well, let me see what I can do. Maybe I can use that as grounds for reconsideration if I can find mistreatment in the facility."

Vegas wasn't too hopeful, but at least that was a start. "Okay, man. Just do what you can and keep me posted."

Vegas exited the building and jumped in his truck. *Damn, I miss her. I got to get her home,* he thought as he headed to the mall.

Once he entered the mall, he went to every jewelry store in search of the perfect wedding band to match my engagement ring. Vegas had asked me to marry him and he was going to make sure he carried through the plan. Nothing was going to stop him, not even jail.

After looking in four jewelry stores, Vegas still had not found the ring he was looking for. He was not expecting such a challenging search. It took no time for him to find the perfect engagement ring, but to find the perfect wedding band was hell. One of the young ladies in the store suggested he have one of my friends help him so that he could have a woman's opinion. Vegas noted her suggestion and called Mickie.

"Yo, Mickie."

"Yeah?"

"This is Vegas. Hey, I need you to help me pick out a ring for C."

"Okay. When you tryin' to look?" Mickie asked, eager to help.

"Well, I started looking today, but I'm gonna look some more tomorrow. I'll give you call."

"A'ight that's cool," Mickie said before hanging up.

After the mall, Vegas made his rounds to all the laundromats and then headed home.

The phone was ringing just as he walked in the door.

"Hello."

"This is a call from inmate—"

Vegas pressed one to accept the call.

"Hey, baby," I said, excited to hear his voice.

"What's up, ma? I spoke to the lawyer today and we're gonna work on getting you outta there. I got big plans for you when you get home. We're gonna make some serious moves."

Vegas sounded excited about the plans he had for the future. I wasn't excited, though. In fact, I wasn't even sure I wanted to come home to him at all. I still hadn't healed from his infidelity, but I made sure I played my cards right. I remained humble and put all the memories of deceit on hold.

"That sounds good, baby. "I just can't wait to get out of here. So, how's life on the streets?" I asked, really not interested in the response. I was sure Vegas was living it up—probably with another woman.

"Shit is lovely, baby. Your house is just like you left it, the laundromats are doing very good and Prissy is still healthy. All I need is you here to make things complete."

"Well, I'm gonna go now. I'll see you Saturday. This time I need you, baby . . . catch my heart."

"I love you, momma," Vegas responded before hanging up the phone.

It was Snake's birthday so Vegas planned a huge party at the crib for him. The hot May weather was perfect for a cookout. Vegas pulled out the grill, Jet Skis, and patio furniture. By nightfall, the party was jumping. Guests included all of my friends, Vegas' boys, and his family. Vegas had a number of tents set up outside. One of the tents was for the women to change into their swimsuits and the other for the men. Vegas also had a special room set up for the birthday boy. This room was for his special gift. Vegas did all he could to keep everyone outside. He really didn't want much traffic inside the house.

As Vegas was bringing the meat outside to put it on the grill, he ran into Mickie.

"What's up, Vegas?" she asked as she walked toward him.

"What's up, Mickie? Who's that you got with you?" Vegas asked as he noticed the very attractive young lady beside Mickie staring at him seductively.

"Oh, I'm sorry. This is Sonya."

"Hi, Sonya," Vegas said as he extended his hand. "You ladies enjoying yourself?" he asked.

"We sure are. Where's your brother?" Mickie asked, unable to locate Snake.

She and Snake had continued their sexual escapade from the night I introduced them at the club. Now things were supposedly serious between them and they were actually calling themselves a couple.

"He's around here somewhere. I'll tell him you're looking for him," Vegas said as he turned his attention back to putting the meat on the grill.

After eating, everyone began to do their own thing. Some people were in the pool, others rode Jet Skis or played cards, and some were dancing. Vegas decided it was time for Snake's grand finale, so he headed out to find him. He looked all over outside, but Snake was nowhere to be found. Vegas decided to head in the house to look for him.

When Vegas walked in the house, he noticed the bedroom door was open. This was odd, because he had made sure to shut all the doors just in case some of the guests wandered in the house. He entered the room slowly. The first section of the room with the Jacuzzi was empty, so he continued to the back where the bed was located.

"Hi, sexy," a female voice sang as Vegas turned the corner. A naked body lay before him. He stood in shock, unable to find any words.

"You like what you see?" the young lady asked as she caressed her clit with one hand and her breasts with the other. Due to the lack of sex Vegas had in the past months, this was an instant arousal.

"Nah, shortie, you got to get the hell out of here," Vegas said, attempting to sound firm.

"Well, from the look of things, you like what you see," the female responded as she looked down toward Vegas' erect penis.

She crawled across the king-size bed toward Vegas, and then she unzipped his pants slowly and pulled out his dick. Vegas tried to resist the temptation, but he was unsuccessful. Her lips were already around his penis and she was giving him crazy brain. Vegas grabbed the back of her head, gripping her long, black hair.

"Ahh . . . ahhhhh . . . ahhhh," he moaned. He was in another world. He was so taken by the head he was getting that he didn't even notice Snake and Mickie standing behind him.

"Sonya!" Mickie yelled. "What the fuck are you doing? Vegas, I can't believe you."

"Ah damn, Mickie. It ain't like that," Vegas tried to explain as Mickie glared at him, shaking her head in disbelief.

"Damn, lil' bro. You doing your thang," Snake said, trying to dap his little brother up. "She gives some good ass head, don't she, man?" Snake continued.

This was beginning to be all too strange to Vegas. "You mean she sucked your dick too, man?"

"Yeah, man. That's our thing. She would have been in there with me and Mickie if you ain't come in and cock block. Me and Mickie were in the bathroom getting our thing on while Sonya was out here getting herself prepared. I always have to get my first nut with my girl, but after that, Sonya comes in and joins us for the second round. She usually likes to listen and play with herself. Sometimes she watches too. All that shit turns her on," Snake explained as if it was nothing out of the ordinary.

"Man, I wasn't even tryin'a fuck with her. She just started sucking my shit. Damn, I fucked up. I fucked up, man." Vegas knew there was no way he could keep Mickie from telling me.

"Fuck it, man. You only live once. R. Kelly thinks he got the best of both worlds. Shit . . . that nigga has no idea." Snake laughed as he smacked Sonya on her ass. "Get dressed. Let's go," Snake said.

After the three of them left the room, Vegas could still picture Mickie shaking her head, a constant reminder of the huge mistake he had made.

Chapter 19
A Turn in the Tables

As Vegas enjoyed life on the outside, I made do with my world behind bars. To utilize my time, I constantly studied law books. I was sure there was some loophole or something that could get me out of jail.

I was no longer in solitary confinement and life in population was better. I didn't need to prove myself. In fact, I had a few chicks who were serving me. My cellmate, Brook, was one of them. She was serving time for embezzlement and had already been turned out in her short stay of only twelve months. She had a huge crush on me, and it was her personal mission to sex me. At times, it was pretty tempting. Brook had a gorgeous shape and a pretty face, unlike most of the females in there. Many of them had million-dollar bodies with food stamp faces.

Brook was my partner in crime. We master-minded a scheme to get me out. With my knowledge in law and her skill at scheming, we came up with the perfect plan. We just had a final few kinks to work out before executing it.

The days began to fly by and Saturday rolled around in the blink of an eye. I anticipated Vegas' arrival. I had a huge surprise for him. I had spoken to Mickie and she told me about his little dick-sucking incident. She told me not to mention it to him and tried to explain how Sonya had provoked him. Of course, none of that really mattered to me. I was able to keep my composure on our calls throughout the week, but I was going to make it my duty to show him a thing or two at visitation. Vegas had fucked me over once and I'd be damned if he was gonna get away with it twice. This was the final straw. I loved Vegas with all my heart and tried with all I had to put things behind me. I knew if I just remained humble, the truth would prevail. I hoped the truth would have been that Vegas really loved me and would never betray me, but deep inside I knew he had turned out to be as much of a snake as his older brother.

"Ceazia Devereaux, visitation!" the deputy called. I took my time walking to the gate. I could see Vegas' nervous smile as I approached.

"Hey, baby," he said as he hugged me tight. I returned a loose hug. My actions were making Vegas uneasy.

"How was your week?" I asked with a mischievous smile. Vegas instantly knew something was up.

"It was cool. What's up with you, C? Why you acting all strange?" he started to ask. That was my cue.

Smack!

I threw my hand across his face.

"Fuck you, Vegas. You just can't seem to keep your dick in your pants, can you?"

It took all he had, but Vegas did not strike back.

"I'm sorry, Ceazia," he said through his teeth. "It was a mistake. I understand if you don't want to be with me anymore, but please just give me a chance to show you I can be the Vegas you've always loved."

"The Vegas I loved protected me, was there for me, loved me, and damn sure never cheated on me," I told him. "I hate you and I never want to see you again." As a final touch, I spit in his face before leaving.

"You're making a mistake, Ceazia!" I could hear him shouting. "You're making a big mistake. Mickie told you what I did, but did she also tell you that she accepted three grand to keep her mouth shut? She's jealous of you, C. She doesn't want us together because she knows how happy you'll be. The bitch is shiesty!"

The pace of my life did a one-hundred and eighty degree turn after that. The days began to move slowly. With Vegas out of my life, I was miserable, but I couldn't continue to be with someone who was unfaithful. He had cheated on me a second time, and that was the final straw. Weeks passed and I did not call Vegas, nor did he come to visit. My mind was torn between Mickie and Vegas.

What if Vegas was telling the truth? Mickie was jeal-

ous of me at one time. Maybe she set the whole thing up. What have I done?

The more I thought about things, the more I wanted Vegas back. My life was empty without him and I wouldn't be whole again until I had my man back in my life. I could no longer bear the pain. Sure, it hurt when I learned of the times he cheated, but the emptiness I felt after we parted seemed never ending. I convinced myself that Vegas deserved another chance. I broke down and called him.

The phone rang, but there was no answer. I found that strange because it was ten in the morning, and Vegas didn't normally get up until after ten. I took that as a sign and left the situation alone. If it were meant to be, we would be reunited somehow.

As the weeks passed, I could feel that I was getting closer and closer to my release. Vegas' lawyer had arranged a hearing for my reconsideration and we definitely had good grounds for release.

"Ceazia Devereaux, please stand for the court's decision," the judge requested. My stomach turned. This was an all too familiar feeling as I waited for another judgment. "I hereby release you into the probation program of Virginia Beach, Virginia."

I could have pissed in my pants. I burst into tears as the words registered.

I'm being released from jail. I can go home. I am finally free.

I left the courtroom on top of the world. There was not a friend, family member, or even Vegas there, but I was still happy.

I thought about how I could go about getting Vegas back as I rode home. The bus ride was long and rough, but nothing could stop the joy I felt. I planned to surprise Vegas. No one knew I was coming home, and that's just the way I wanted it. Sure, Vegas had really done some terrible things, but I had forgiven him. After days and days of soul searching, I figured there were too many what-ifs and I decided to give Vegas the benefit of the doubt. I figured all the ups and downs throughout our relationship would only make us stronger. He had asked me to be his wife, and I had every intention of being just that.

From the bus station, I took a cab to my house. The house was big and beautiful, just as I remembered it. I really missed home. A huge smile came across my face as I pressed the digits of my birth date on the keypad and the gate opened. I walked to the door slowly. I didn't want Vegas to hear me enter.

I became more and more anxious the closer I got to the bedroom. I could hear the jets blowing in the Jacuzzi. I figured Vegas was probably relaxing after a long workout. He would often do that when I was home. I cracked the door just enough to peep in. The vision before me would never leave my mind. There were Vegas, Mickie, and Sonya all ass-naked in my Jacuzzi, sniffing cocaine. I stood frozen in my tracks. I didn't know what to do. I managed to back away from the door without being noticed and proceeded to walk to the basement in a trance. When I got to the bottom step, I reached on top of the water heater and it was there, just as I had left it. My gun had not been moved. I loaded the gun slowly as tears escaped the confines of my eyelids and rolled down my face. This was the final deceit.

I walked back to the bedroom and opened the door. They were so high that they didn't even notice my presence. I watched Vegas laying back in enjoyment as Sonya sucked his dick and Mickie rubbed all over his body. I couldn't believe she would stoop so low.

Bang . . . bang . . . bang . . . bang!

They had no idea what hit them. The room was silent. No screams were ever heard. I watched as the Jacuzzi waters quickly turned red. Vegas, however, was not yet dead.

"Ceazia, I'm sorry, baby," he whispered as blood streamed down the side of his face. "I'm sorry. I'll always love you. Catch my heart."

Those were the last words Vegas spoke before his eyes closed to an eternal sleep. His words pierced my heart.

Vegas . . . what have I done? I've killed the love of my life. My brain was racing. *How can I live without him? Vegas, wake up! Please, wake up!*

I shook his body frantically, but he did not move. His body lay still. I screamed in pain. Vegas was gone and I had killed him.

I fixed myself a drink and walked over to my bed. And this is where I've been ever since.

So, you may be wondering why I'm telling you this story. Just to instill a single thought:

For what is a man profited if he shall gain the whole world and lose his own soul? Or what shall a man give in exchange for his soul?
Matthew 16:26

Look for Chunichi's new book

Married to the Game

Chapter 1

"Who says I got to stay in your house?"

"*Bam!*"
I slammed the door behind me as I rushed outside.

"I hate you!"

I screamed upstairs to my aunt who's had custody of me for the past 10 years. My mother was doing time in the Virginia's Women's State Prison for child neglect. One night after a three day stay at the crack house she came home frustrated and shook my little brother to death. She would often come home fiendin' once her monthly welfare check was gone. This particular time she was so sick that the constant cry of my five-month-old brother drove her insane. I was hiding under the table in our dark house that was lit by candles only because we had no electricity. I remember my mom yelling,

"Shut up, boy! Shut up!" as she shook my brother until he was silent. Once he was quiet, she laid him on the mattress that we had for a bed. She then pulled out a cigarette and laid on the couch. It wasn't until then I felt safe enough to come out. I crawled into the bedroom and laid beside my little brother. I cried silently as I touched his still hand.

"Wake up, little Jay. Wake up," I whispered. But there was no response. I wrapped my arm around his little body and fell asleep.

"*Beep . . . bbeeeppp . . . bbbbbeeeeppppppp . . .*"

I woke to see red, orange, and yellow flames all around me. I panicked once I realized I couldn't breathe.

"Mommy . . . mommy!"

I yelled frantically as I felt my way to the back door. Outside I saw the ambulance and all my neighbors, but my mom wasn't out there nor my little brother. As soon as the firemen pulled up, I begged them to save my brother and mother. Within minutes they were out. They both lay still as the paramedics tried to resuscitate them. My mom came around shortly but my brother was covered with a white blanket. That was my signal that he was gone. Everyone figured it was from smoke inhalation but I knew the truth. To this day, no one knows that my mommy really killed little Jay. That will be a secret I'll take to my grave. The only reason my mom was arrested was for child neglect. The neighbors had reported her a number of times and this time when she fell asleep with the cigarette lit, it was the last straw. It didn't take long for the paramedics to realize she was high. She got sentenced to the Women's State Prison for 15 years and that's where she's been for the past 10 years. In those years I've blossomed from a timid four year old tot to a rebellious teen.

"If you hate it here so bad, then leave!" My aunt

yelled after me. I could hear her coming down the stairs as her yells got louder.

"Where you gonna go? Don't nobody else want you," she continued to yell as she opened the screen door.

"I hate it here. I'd rather be dead than live here with you," I shouted back. I knew that response was only going to lead to one thing, but I was so sick of the foul treatment I didn't even care.

"*Smack!*"

My aunt's huge hand swept across my face.

"You better watch your damn mouth, little girl. You getting a little too hot for your pants." I jumped up without thinking and smacked her right back. In a matter of seconds my aunt's 250 pound frame was all over me. I screamed hoping my grandmother would come to my rescue.

"Gggggrrrrraaaaaannnddddddmmmmmmaaaaa! Help! She's trying to kill me," I yelled.

My grandmother was out the door and pulling my aunt off me in no time. I was big for my size, but my 135 pound frame was nothing compared to the strength of that beast. I rushed upstairs to my room as soon as I was free.

"I'm packing my bags!" I shouted as I ran up the stairs. I pulled out my Jansport backpack and stuffed it with toiletries, underclothes, a pair of daisy duke jean shorts, a white wife beater, slouch socks, and a fresh pair of white Air Force Ones. I planned to stay at my girl, Gina's, house. Her mom worked the overnight shift, 7 p.m. to 7 a.m., at the hospital so we would always have a ball at her house. It was right around six o'clock so I knew her mom would already be out the crib and on her way to work.

"I'm out," I yelled one last time as I ran back down the stairs.

"BJ!" I could hear my grandma yelling. That was the nick name the family had given me. My name is actually Jasmine and everyone called me Jay, but when my brother was born he was named Javon and we called him Jay too. So to distinguish who was who, they began calling us big Jay and little Jay. Eventually big Jay turned into BJ.

"Yes grandma?" I stopped at the back door to hear her out.

"Don't go out there getting in trouble, ya hear?"

"Okay grandma. I'll call you."

I loved my grandmother and hated for her to worry, but I just had to do me for the time being. I exited out the back door and jumped the fence. A couple of blocks later I was in the projects. I was cautious as I walked to Gina's place. I was out of my territory and there were a lot of chicks that didn't like me out there. I dominated the 8th grade with my fully developed body. Needless to say, not too many girls liked it when their boyfriends lusted over me.

'Bang . . . bang . . . bang!"

I knocked on Gina's front door. I knew she wouldn't be able to hear me because I could hear the music blasting from her bedroom window.

"Yo, Gina!" I unsuccessfully attempted to get her attention. I tried the obvious and twisted the door knob. "Wha-la!"

Like magic the door was open. This chick didn't even have the door locked. I crept up the stairs planning to scare the hell out of her. When I got to her door I busted in.

"Aaaahhhhh!" we both screamed at the top of our lungs.

"Oh my God Gina. What the hell are you doing?"

Gina jumped up pulling the covers over her naked body. The smell of sex and weed filled the room. I laughed at her and Duke as they both struggled to get dressed. Duke was a friend of ours since elementary. He was 16 and in high school. He and Gina always argued and fought with each other. I had no idea they were doing the nasty.

"Ah-ha! I blew y'all's spot up! I knew something was up with y'all. Ain't no way in hell two people could hate each other as much or as long as y'all two," I said as I continued to laugh. I noticed Gina didn't think it was funny at all.

"Why didn't you knock first? How the fuck you just going to run up in my shit, BJ?"

Gina got on the defensive. I figured she was embarrassed that her secret was out. I became kind of jealous myself. I had no idea she was having sex. Duke took his time getting dressed. I noticed him eyeballing my breasts as he massaged his penis. I gave him a seductive grin and returned the favor as I eyeballed his nice size penis. Gina quickly interrupted our flirting session.

"Duke, I think you should leave. I'll call you later," Gina said.

Duke agreed without a fight.

"Aight, momma," he said before kissing her on the cheek and exiting the room. He gave me one last glance and a nod of the head.

"Bye, Duke," I said, grinning. Now it was time for me to confront Gina.

"I always thought we both were virgins and when we decided to have sex we would let each other know. Why didn't you tell me, Gina?" Gina looked away as she answered.

"I haven't been a virgin for a long time, BJ, but it was out of my control. I wish I could tell you more about it, but I can't."

I could see Gina wipe the tears from her eyes. I hugged her tightly.

"You can tell me anything, Gina. I won't think any differently of you. You're my girl."

I tried to reassure her as we talked. Gina still refused to share. I figured it was either too embarrassing or too hurtful for her to share, so I left the situation alone and allowed her to cry. After minutes of silent tears Gina finally spoke.

"It was Bubba, BJ. It was Bubba," She forced the words out between a huge cry. Bubba was Gina's mother's boyfriend. I couldn't believe what my ears were hearing.

"Bubba? You had sex with Bubba?" I asked.

"Yes. One night he came home after the club drunk. Of course my mom was at work so I was here alone. He came in my room and started to pull my pajamas off and forcing his hands inside me. . . ."

Gina stopped in the middle of her statement and began to cry. It was too unbearable to speak about.

"It's okay, Gina. You don't have to say anymore."

I hugged her. I could feel her pain. I never experienced being raped, but I'm sure it has to be a painful experience.

"He raped me, BJ. He raped me and my mother called me a liar when I told her about it. I don't know what hurt more, the rape or my mother's disbelief."

I had no idea Gina had so much pain and hurt inside. There were no words that could heal the pain she felt, so instead of speaking, I just listened and consoled her as she released all the misery she held inside. The room was silent as we sat on her bed. I listened to her constant sniffle as I rubbed her back.

Chapter 2

"I'm a little soldier in training"

Sex with Gina is always good, but I would really like to hit BJ. I can tell she wants me from the way she looks at me. She's still a virgin, but her pussy is steaming for some sex. I'm not going to rush it though. I know I'll hit it. I'm a Jackson man and we're known for getting any female we want. My uncles, Vegas and Snake, together ran all the ladies before Vegas was killed. In fact, it's his womanizing ways that got him murdered. I plan to follow right in their footsteps but I'll be a little wiser with mine. I get constant training from my uncle Snake. He keeps me tight in all the hottest gear and jewelry. He even bought me a car before I had a license. Snake always refers to me as his little soldier in training. Tonight we'll be covering strip club etiquette.

I arrived at Snake's house around 10 o'clock. I was greeted at the door by his girl, Danielle. Danielle was this bourgeois chick my uncle met at Hampton University. Her mother's a doctor and father's a lawyer. She has never been exposed to the streets and that's what she loves about Snake; his spontaneous bad boy traits. Danielle was definitely a dime piece. She had a small waist with a big ass, just the way I like them.

"What's up, Danielle?" I asked as I admired her booty on the way in.

"Hey, Duke. What's going on?" she asked, wondering what the night might bring.

"I don't know, momma. I think we're going to hit the strip joint up tonight."

Danielle hated when Snake went to the strip club. All she could think about was the sexual rendezvous he used to have with his stripper ex-girlfriend, Mickie, and her female lover, Sonya, who was a stripper as well. The shit my uncles used to do back in the day was wild. No one likes to talk about it, because it was a deadly love triangle, but me; I love it and plan to live it.

"Oh, you're going to the strip club tonight, Snake?" Danielle immediately asked him.

"Nah, baby. I don't know why you always let lil' soldier get in your head. He knows you hate it when I go there and that's why he said the shit."

Snake spit game to her as he took his last pull on the blunt. It was amazing how easy it was to turn things around in a matter of seconds. Running game was a science and I had almost mastered it as good as my uncle.

"Damn, Danielle, I didn't know you let a young nigga like me get in your head like that. My uncle better watch out," I said with a smirk on my face. Danielle was not pleased with our taunting. She rolled her eyes and began to clean up the small mess my uncle left behind.

"We out, baby," Snake said as he kissed his girl on the lips. She walked with us to the door. I could see the frame of her thong through her sheer robe. I smacked her ass on the way out.

"We out, baby." I said, mocking my uncle Snake. They both laughed. But it wasn't a joke at all. I was planning to fuck that fat ass from the back one day soon. It may take a while, but I'll get it and Danielle knew it. I winked my eye at her and grabbed my dick before closing the door behind me.

We jumped in Snake's Denali and headed to the strip club. I was a little excited but I knew I had to play it cool. As we pulled up to the club, I followed Snake past the security and into the club. That was the first lesson. I made a mental note.

Get familiar with the security. Give them a nice amount of cash to avoid lines and searching.

Once we were inside, the first stop was the bar. Snake took a spot in the corner and handed the bartender a generous amount of money.

"Courvoisier, and keep 'em coming," he told the bartender. That was two lessons in one. Snake walked right in without much noise and headed to a spot in the corner. This was so that he could check out the scene. You must always be aware of your environment so that there aren't any surprises. Next he paid the bartender up front and a generous amount. That keeps him from having the hassle of flagging down the bartender and constantly having to order. We chilled in the corner for about 45 minutes. At first that was cool because I was checking out some of the amazing things those chicks could do on that pole, but after a while that was no longer holding my attention.

Females were coming over left and right and Snake was turning them down. Now that part of the lesson I didn't grasp at all.

"Unc, why you dissing all the honies?" I asked.

"A couple of reasons, man. First, some of them are tricks and we don't do tricks. And second, if you ignore them and act uninterested towards the hot bitches, the challenge is going to make them want you even more. You see the hot bitches are used to getting any nigga they come at. If you're that one nigga that don't budge, then they're going to want you even more. You feel me lil' nigga?"

My uncle was so good with game it was ridiculous. Everything he said made perfect sense.

"I feel you, Unc. I feel ya."

We continued to chill at the bar for another 20 minutes before Snake led me to the velvet room. Shit in there was set up like a little Egyptian paradise and the women were beautiful, nothing but top notch females. It was one female in particular that kept looking our way. She was the baddest chick in there. She had beautiful caramel skin, a small waist, C cup breasts and long black hair. Snake noticed me checking her out.

"You like that?" he asked as he waited for a reaction. I was sure not to seem too pressed.

"So far she's the baddest chick I've seen in here," I carefully responded.

"Each day you show more and more traits of your uncle Vegas," my uncle said as he laughed. He shook his head as if to say: It's a pity.

"She's venomous, man. That's the infamous Ceazia," he said as he looked her 5 foot 5 inch frame up and down.

"Damn, that's her? She doesn't look much like a murderer to me," I said as I watched her move her body like a snake. Her panther eyes had me hypnotized as she walked over.

"Who's this little one, Snake?" she asked while rubbing her hand across my goatee.

"Nobody you getting close to, bitch," Snake snapped at her. It had never been proven that she was the shooter the day Vegas, Mickie, and Sonya were killed, but Snake was sure she did it.

"Don't be jealous, Daddy, you'll always have my attention," she said to Snake as she rubbed his penis. Snake didn't respond, he just looked her coldly in her eyes.

I constantly watched Ceazia throughout the night. The spell she had on the men in the club was crazy. I knew she had to be making the most bank in the whole club. There wasn't a flaw on her body. Her skin was perfect, stomach tight, not a stretch mark in sight, and she had perfect white teeth. She was truly a stunna. No wonder my uncle Vegas was whipped. Pretty soon I plan to see just how much we really have in common.